D1325485

The Laughing
Academy

Shena Mackay

THE
LAUGHING
ACADEMY

HEINEMANN : LONDON

First published in Great Britain 1993
by William Heinemann Ltd
an imprint of Reed Consumer Books Ltd
Michelin House, 81 Fulham Road, London SW3 6RB
and Auckland, Melbourne and Singapore

Reprinted 1993

'A Mine of Serpents' was commissioned by BBC Radio 4
and broadcast on 5 November 1991, and first published
in *Telling Stories 2* (ed. Duncan Minshull), Coronet 1993

'The New Year Boy' was commissioned by BBC Radio 4
and broadcast on 1 January 1992.

'A Pair of Spoons' was first published in slightly different
form in *Critical Quarterly*, vol. 32, no. 1, spring 1990,
and subsequently in *Best Short Stories 1991*, (ed. Giles Gordon
and David Hughes), William Heinemann, 1991.

'Glass' was previously published in *Femme de Siècle*
(ed. Joan Smith), Chatto & Windus, 1992.

'The Curtain With the Knot In It' was first published
in *Midwinter Mysteries* (ed. Hilary Hale),
Little, Brown & Co., 1992

'Two Sleepy People' by Hogey Carmichael and Frank Loesser
© 1938 Famous Music Corp. USA.
Famous Chappell/International Music Publications.
Used by permission.

'For All We Know' by Samuel Lewis and Fred Coots
used by kind permission of Redwood Music Ltd, Iron Bridge House,
3 Bridge Approach, Chalk Farm, London, NW1 8BD.

A CIP catalogue record for this title
is available from the British Library
ISBN 0 434 44047 7

Printed and bound in Great Britain
by Clays Ltd, St Ives plc

To Morag Mackey,
née Carmichael, 1918–1992

With special thanks to Rebecca Brown
for her word-processing assistance.

Contents

A Pair of Spoons

Villagers passing the Old Post Office were stopped in their tracks by a naked woman dancing in the window. Not quite naked, for she wore a black straw hat dripping cherries and a string of red glass beads which made her white nudity more shocking. When they perceived that the figure behind the dusty glass was a dummy, a mannequin or shop-front model, they quickened their steps, clucking, peevish and alarmed like the pheasants that scurried down the lane and disappeared through the hedge. After a while only visitors to the village hidden in a fold of the Herefordshire hills, those who had parked their cars outside Minimarket and, seduced by the stream with its yellow irises and dragonflies, had wandered along the grassy bank that ran down one side of the lane, were struck by the nude with cherry hat and beads, frozen in mid-dance by their scandalised stares.

The Old Post Office, which used to do business from the double-fronted room jutting out into the lane, had stood empty for several years following the death of the retired postmaster. Posters advertising National Savings, warning against the invasion of the Colorado beetle, and depicting heroic postmen struggling to the outposts of the Empire still hung on the walls, curled and faded to the disappointing pinks, yellows, greens and blues of a magic painting book, while stamps and pensions were dispensed and bureaucratic rituals were enacted now through a

1

grille of reinforced plastic at the back of Minimarket. In that shop window was a notice board and prominent among the advertisements for puppies, firewood, machine-knitted garments and sponsored fun-runs, walks, swims and bake-ins, was a card which read in antiqued scrolly script: We buy Old Gold, Silver, Pewter, Brass and Broken Jewellery, any condition. China, Clocks, Furniture, Books, Comics, Tin Toys, Dinkies, Matchbox etc., Lead Farm Animals, Clothes, Victoriana, Edwardiana, Bijouterie. Houses Cleared. Best Prices. Friendly Old-Established Firm. Ring us on 634 and we will call with No Obligation.

Parts of the Old Post Office house predated the four-teenth-century church whose clock and mossy graves could be seen from the kitchen window through a tangle of leggy basil plants on the sill above the stone sink. Anybody peeping in on a summer evening would have seen the Old-Established Firm, Vivien and Bonnie, sharp-featured and straight-backed, tearing bread, keeping an eye on each other's plates, taking quick mouthfuls with a predatory air as if they had poached the pasta under the gamekeeper's eye; two stoats sitting up to table. Their neat hindquarters, in narrow jeans, rested on grubby embroidered cushions set with bits of broken mirror and sequins which overlapped the seats of the Sheraton-style fruitwood chairs; they rested their elbows on a wormy Jacobean table whose wonky leg was stabilised by a copy of *Miller's Antiques Prices Guide*. It was Vivien, with her art-school training, who had calligraphed the notice in the village shop: after meeting Bonnie, she had taken a crash course in English porcelain and glass. Bonnie relied on the instinct which had guided her when she started out as an assistant on a stall in the Portobello Road, where she had become expert in rubbing dust into the rough little flowers and fleeces and faked crazed-glaze of reproduction shepherdesses, goatherds, cupidons, lambs

2

and spaniels, and which had taken her to co-owner of this ever-appreciating pile of bricks and beams. Vivien and Bonnie moved through Antiques Fayres like weasels in a hen house. To their fellow dealers they were known, inevitably, as Bonnie and Clyde, or the Terrible Twins.

At night they slept curved into each other in their blue sheets like a pair of spoons in a box lined with dusty blue velvet, or with stained pink silk in summer: two spoons, silver-gilt a little tarnished by time, stems a little bent, which would realise less than half of their value if sold singly rather than as a pair.

They had grown more alike through the years since they had been married in a simple ceremony at the now-defunct and much-lamented Gateways club. How to tell them apart? Vivien bore a tiny scar like a spider-crack on glass on her left cheekbone, the almost invisible legacy of the party that followed their nuptials, where Bonnie's former lover had thrown a glass of wine in her face. Or had it been Vivien's rejected girlfriend? Nobody could remember now, least of all the person who had flung the wine.

'Vivien is more vivid, and Bonnie's bonnier,' suggested a friend when the topic of their similarity was raised.

'No, it's the other way round,' another objected.

'A bit like dog owners turning into their dogs . . .'

'But who is the dog, and who the owner?'

'Now you're being bitchy.'

That conversation, which took place in London, would have struck an uneasy chord of recognition in Vivien had it been transmitted over the miles. She had become aware of an invisible lead attached to her collar and held kindly but firmly in Bonnie's hand. There were days when she seemed as insubstantial as Bonnie's shadow; she became aware that she mirrored Bonnie's every action. Bonnie took off her sweater, Vivien took off hers; Bonnie reached for her green and gold tobacco tin; Vivien took out her

3

own cigarette papers; Bonnie felt like a coffee, so did Vivien and they sipped in unison; Bonnie ground pepper on to her food and Vivien held out her hand for the mill; when Bonnie, at the wheel of the van, pulled down her sun visor, Vivien's automatic hand reached up and she confronted her worried face in the vanity mirror. At night when they read in bed the pages of their books rasped in synchronicity until Bonnie's light clicked off and then Vivien's pillow was blacked out as suddenly as a tropical sky at sunset.

'You go on reading, love, if you want to. It won't disturb me.'

'No, I'm shattered,' replied Vivien catching Bonnie's yawn, and swallowing it as the choke-chain tightened around her throat. The next morning, noticing that her Marmite soldier had lined up in the precise formation of Bonnie's troop, she pushed her plate away.

'Do you think you could manage on your own today? I don't feel so good.'

'You do look a bit green round the gills. I hope you're not coming down with something.'

Bonnie laid one hand on Vivien's brow and with the other appropriated her toast.

'You haven't got a temperature.'

'Well I feel funny.'

'We're supposed to be going to pick up that grand-mother clock from that old boy, and there's the car boot sale – oh well, I suppose I *can* go on my own . . . hope to Christ he hasn't done anything stupid like having it valued, you can't trust those old buzzards, dead crafty, some of them . . .'

Their two egg shells lay on her polished plate, hardly damaged, sucked clean by a nifty rodent.

Vivien guided the van out into the lane; Bonnie had taken off one of the gates on the rearside wing once when she was cross. Vivien waved her off and watched the dust settle. She felt an immediate surge of energy and fuelled it with a doorstep of toast spread with honey found in the cupboard of a house they had cleared, crunching on the cells of a comb rifled from the hive by the fingers of a dead woman. The bees had all buzzed off by the time Bonnie and Vivien had hacked their way through the tangled garden, and the empty wooden hives, weathered to grey silk, stood now in their cobbled yard.

Vivien left her sticky plate and knife in the sink and, sucking sweetness from her teeth, locked the door and set off down the lane with a wave to the woman dancing in the window. The vicar, passing by on the other side, ducked his head in the cold nod that was the most, in charity, that he need vouchsafe the Londoners since Bonnie had made him an offer for the paten and chalice.

'Morning, vicar. Lovely morning, isn't it? Makes you feel good to be alive,' Vivien called out uncharacteristically, surprising them both.

The incumbent was forced to look at her across the lane, a skinny lumberjack cramming into her mouth a spray of the redcurrants which hung like cheap glass beads among the fuchsias in her red and purple raggedy hedge, and caught a glitter of glass flashing crimson fire on plastic flesh, and a dangle of cherries.

'Hedge could do with a trim,' he said.

'Oh, we like it like that,' reminding him that she was half of the dubious duo. She was sucking the end of a honeysuckle trumpet. At this rate she wouldn't need the hedge trimmer he had been about to offer. She would soon have eaten the whole hedge.

'Ah well,' he concluded.

His skirt departed to the east and Vivien's jeans loped westward. She was trying to suppress the little maggot of anxiety whose mealy mouth warned that Bonnie might telephone to find out how she was. As she passed the call-box she had such a vivid image of Bonnie impotently misting up the glass panes of an identical construction standing among moon daisies on a grassy verge, while the phone rang and rang in their empty kitchen, that she could only assume that telepathy was at work. She thought, and walked on, stopping outside a garden at a box of worm-eaten windfalls with 'Please help yourselves' scrawled on a piece of cardboard. Vivien filled her pockets. She came to a gate, placed one hand on the topmost bar and vaulted into a field of corn, and followed a natural track through the furrows, now spitting husks and crunching sweet kernels, now negotiating an apple, until she was faced with barbed wire and a ditch of nettles. She stood wavering wildly on the wire and hurled herself forward, landing, with only the softest malevolent graze of leaves on her bare ankles, in a field whose hay had been harvested, leaving its scent in the air. The field was bordered on three sides by massive trees, oak, sycamore, ash, chestnut, and although it was only July, recent rain had brought down a scattering of tiny green conkers. 'Like medieval fairies' weapons', thought Vivien, whose fancy, when not stamped on by Bonnie, flew on such flights, 'those spiked balls on chains.' Aluminium animal troughs rusted in a heap. At the far end of the field was a gate set in a high hedge and Vivien walked towards it dreamily with the sun freckling her face and her arms beneath her rolled-up sleeves.

The latch lifted but she had to force the gate against hanks of long grass, and squeeze herself through the gap. She was at the edge of a garden and now she saw a house which was not visible from the field. Old glass in the windows glittered like insects' wings. No dog barked. The house exuded emptiness, shimmering in the heat haze while housemartins flew in and out of their shells of honeycombed mud under the eaves. As she walked over the lawn she realised that the grass here had been cut not very long ago: it was springy beneath her feet, studded with purple milkwort and daisies and buttercups that seemed to acknowledge the futility of growing too tall. Somebody, therefore, cared for the garden. The roses needed to be deadheaded, the petals were falling from the irises and peonies revealing shiny seed cases, but apart from the soggy roses and a faint mist here and there of lesser willowherb and an occasional intrusive cow parsley and weedy seedling brought up by the rain, the flowerbeds were orderly. She meant only to peep through the windows.

It was strange, she thought, as she walked on rose petals round the back ground-floor windows, pressing her face against the old dark glass, how she did not feel like a trespasser, but as though she had inadvertently locked herself out of those rooms hung with faded velvet curtains and had the right to walk on the pale carpets and curl up in that yellow velvet chair with a blond dog at her feet. She stared at old wooden kitchen cupboards holding china and utensils behind their half-open sliding doors, the mottle enamel gas cooker, the pyramidal iron saucepan stand, the fossilised pink soap and rusty brillo pad on the draining board, the clean tea towels, bleached and brittle as ancient flags. A movement by her foot made her look down. A toad regarded her with amber eyes. She crouched before it and reached out to pick it up. The toad leaped for the dank shadow under a flat scratchy plant. Vivien thrust her fingers after it and scrabbled in dead leaves and needles. Instead of pulsating skin, she struck metal. She drew out a key. It came as no surprise that the key fitted the lock of the scullery door, and turned, through cobwebs and flakes of rust, to admit her to the stone-flagged floor. The mangle, the stone sink, the disconnected twin-tub, had been waiting for her.

Vivien moved through the rooms, acknowledging the pile of enamel dogs' dishes in the kitchen, the Chinese umbrella stand holding walking sticks, knobkerries and a brace of Union Jacks, the wellies sealed with cobwebs, the waterpoof coats and jackets on the pegs, the polished tallboys, chests of drawers, the empty vases, the glass-fronted cabinets holding miniatures and enamelled boxes, scent bottles and figurines, the groves of books, the quiet beds, the framed photographs, the high dry baths, the box spilling shoes. Everywhere she saw herself reflected, framed in elaborate gilt on the walls, elongated in tilted cheval glasses, in triplicate and thence to infinity above dressing tables, dimly in the glass of pictures. She touched nothing. At last she let herself out again, locked the scullery door, and put the key in her pocket.

'The state of you!' Bonnie scolded. 'Where've you *been*? I've been back for an hour. I rang to see how you were but there was no reply . . .'

'Just for a walk. I needed some air.'

'You could have got that in the garden.' Bonnie waved an arm at the sofa spewing horsehair onto the cobbles.

'It's damp and smelly,' Vivien protested. 'Did you get the clock?'

'No, I didn't.' Bonnie brushed grimly at grass seeds and burrs clinging to Vivien's clothes. 'You look as if you've been rolling in the hay. Have you?'

'Chance would be a fine thing. Ouch.'

The village maidens had a tendency to obesity and anoraks and, this summer, fluorescent shorts. Bonnie slapped at Vivien's jeans, reactivating the nettle stings. Stung into memory of her first sights of the house, and walking again in its peaceful rooms, Vivien half-heard Bonnie's voice.

'. . . decided not to part with it for sentimental reasons, lying old toad, then he let slip that he'd heard the Antiques Roadshow might be coming round next year . . . thought I'd really cracked it . . . who did he think he was kidding, you could practically see him rehearsing the greedy smile of wonderment that would light up his toothless old chops when they told him his crappy clock was worth a small fortune . . . I'd like to tear up his bus pass, he practically promised me . . . sell their own grand-mothers, these people . . .'

'I thought that was precisely what he wouldn't do?' Vivien returned to the present.

'What?'

'Sell his grandmother. Clock.'

'*Don't* try to be clever, it doesn't suit you.'

I am clever, thought Vivien, and it might suit me very well.

'Shall we go to the pub later?' she said.

'No. What do you want to go there for? I thought we agreed that the ambiente was nonsimpatico?'

'Well, yes. I just thought you might fancy going out for a change.'

Vivien ripped the ring-pulls from two cold beers from the fridge and handed one to Bonnie. It was true that the pub was uncongenial. The locals were a cliquey lot. Bonnie could take off their accent brilliantly. 'Oooh-arr' she had riposted to those guys' offer to buy them a drink, and suddenly she and Vivien were on the outside of a circle of broad backs. No sense of humour. And boring – most of their conversation was limited to the agricultural; there were so many overheard references to filling in dykes that the girls could not but feel uneasy, especially as those ditches were not a feature of the local landscape. Aggression flared in wet patches in the armpits and on the bulging bellies scarcely contained in T-shirts that bobbed like balloons along the bar. The landlord, who was in the early stages of vegetabliasis – so far his nose had turned into an aubergine – snarled at them, as if he thought they would turn the beer.

9

'Let's go and sit in the garden,' said Vivien, leading the way. 'How was the car boot sale?'

'Like a car boot sale.'

They ate outside, sucking little bones and tossing them against the rising moon, straining their eyes in the dusk to pick out their autumn wardrobe from the L.L. Bean catalogue, and going into the house only when it grew too dark to read even by moonlight and starlight, and it was time to luxuriate with a nightcap in the pleasures of *Prisoner: Cell Block H*, propped up in bed by pillows, in front of the television. Long after Bonnie had fallen asleep, whimpering slightly as if dreaming of chasing rabbits, Vivien lay awake with a glass-fronted cabinet glowing in the dark before her eyes. A slight flaw or bend in the glass gave a mocking, flirtatious twist to the rosy lips of the porcelain boy in a yellow jacket and pink breeches, ruffled in a gentle breeze the green feather in his red hat, lifted the wings of the bird in his hands, and raised an eyebrow at the little girl clutching a wriggling piglet against her low-cut laced bodice over a skirt striped with flowers. A black and gold spotted leopard with a pretty face and gold-tipped paws lounged benignly between them, and putti, half-decorously wreathed, offered baskets of flowers.

Vivien, falling into sleep, put her hand out in the moonlight and found that the cabinet had no key. The moon hung between the open curtains like a huge battered gold coin almost within her grasp.

A week passed before Vivien could return to her house. At the wheel of the van, at the kitchen cooker, in dusty halls where people haggled over trinkets and dead people's clothes and crazed enamel hairbrushes and three-tiered cake stands, she cherished her secret. Had she asked herself why, she might have replied that it was because it was the only secret she had ever held from Bonnie; or

10

she might have said that for the first time she wanted to look at and touch beautiful objects without putting a price on them, or even that there was something in the air of the house that stayed her hand from desecration, but she was careful not to ask herself any questions. Once or twice she caught Bonnie giving her a look. They slept uneasily, with bad dreams of one another.

It happened that Bonnie had to attend a surprise family party for her parents' Golden Wedding. The anticipation of the celebration, where she would stand as a barren fig tree among the Laura Ashley floribunda and fecundity, put her in such a black mood that Vivien expired a long sigh of relief, as if anxiety had been expelled from her by the despairing farewell toot, as the van lurched like a tumbrel into the lane. The golden present, exquisitely encased in gold foil, with gold ribbon twirled to curlicues round a pencil to disguise its essential tackiness, had been wrapped by Vivien but her name did not appear on the gold gift tag. Bonnie's Russian wedding ring and the true lover's knot, the twin of that which circled Vivien's little finger, would dissolve into invisibility when she crossed the family threshold. An uncle would prod her stomach and tell her she ought to get some meat on her bones, a man likes something he can get hold of; a sister-in-law, made bold by Malibu and cake, might enquire after Bonnie's flatmate while rearranging by a fraction of an inch her own present of a pair of gilded ovals framing studio portraits of gap-toothed grandchildren. Later the same sister-in-law would offer on a stained paper plate the stale and indigestible news that she had once been disconcerted by a desire to kiss a schoolfriend, and on the homeward journey the memory of her confession would jolt into her stomach and the motorway verge would receive a shower of shame and disgust for the unnatural recipient of her secret. Meanwhile, however, Bonnie was

11

being introduced to the fiancé of a niece, who was omitting her name from his mental list of wedding guests even as they shook hands.

'You might have made the effort to put on a skirt for once,' her mother told her. In fact, Bonnie and Vivien did occasionally outrage their friends by wearing skirts. The last time had been when they turned up at the Treacle Pudding Club in a heat wave in their batiks and had been refused entry, but she didn't tell her mother this. Bonnie went into the garden and made herself a roll-up.

'You'll die if you smoke,' said a small boy in a red waistcoat with matching bow tie on elastic.

'Want a drag?' Bonnie held out the cigarette.

He shook his head so hard that his eyes rolled like blue doll's eyes, as if they would fall out, and ran in to report the death threat, and shot her with a plastic machine-gun from an upstairs window. Bonnie looked at her watch, reflecting with relief that the late-night, half-hearted discussions with Vivien about adoption, early in their marriage, had fizzled away with the morning Alka-Seltzer. If they *had* been allowed to adopt one, they would have had to have it adopted. She went in to the telephone on the public shelf above the hall radiator and dialled home, clamping the receiver to her ear to keep out the sounds of merry making, the mouth piece poised to muffle her low desperate 'Hi babe, it's me. Just needed to hear your voice'; words that she was to be deprived of muttering. No comfort came from the shrilling 1940s handset in the Old Post Office kitchen and, blinded by a paper hat which someone had slipped over her head, she went back to join the party.

'I rang. You weren't there,' she said as she slammed the van door and strode past Vivien who had run to meet her, into the house.

'Is that my doggie bag?' Vivien pulled at the purple

12

Liberty carrier in Bonnie's hand. 'What have you brought me?'

'Nothing. You didn't deserve anything. I ate it in the van. Where were you, when I needed you?'

Vivien might have replied, 'I was in my house, perfectly happy. I was reading, grazing among the books, and walking in the garden, and suddenly I thought of the hard little face, the mean mouth that I fell in love with, and I came running home.'

She said, 'I went for a walk, babe. I was very lonesome all by my little self, without you.'

Bonnie, half-placated, dropped the bag on to the table. 'There's a bit of cake left.'

Vivien drew it out.

'You've eaten off the icing. You pig.'

'Yes,' said Bonnie sternly.

'What's this?' Vivien scrabbled in Bonnie's bag and pulled out by the leg a mothy-looking toy.

'My old teddy. It's so threadbare I thought we could pass it off as Victorian. They're fetching a good price now.'

'Oh Bonnie, you can't sell him, he's cute. Look at his little beady eyes.'

'Give it here. I'll pull one off, make it even cuter – nothing more poignant than a sad teddy, is there?'

'No! I won't let you. How could you be so cruel? I'm going to keep him. He's probably your oldest friend . . .'

. . . A tiny Bonnie, rosy from her bath, toddled up the wooden hill to Bedfordshire, holding a sleepy teddy by the paw . . .

'Actually she's a girl. Tedina. I used to smack her with my hairbrush.'

Vivien thought a flicker of fear passed over Tedina's tiny black eyes. She rooted in a box and found a Victorian christening robe.

13

'Perfect,' said Bonnie. 'Fifty quid at least.'

'There's a fatal flaw in your plan,' Viven told her. 'Teddy bears weren't invented in Victorian times.'

'Don't be stupid. Of course they were. Albert brought one back from Germany or something one Christmas. They're called after him.' Sensing a flaw in her argument, if not in her plan, Bonnie let the subject drop. Tedina, in her white pin-tucked robe was carried upstairs to their bed by Vivien and the hairbrush, a section of the carapace of a dead tortoise set in silver, was put tactfully in a drawer.

It was when she picked up the local paper that she saw an unmistakable photograph, the notice that read 'House for Sale By Auction with contents'. She stuffed the paper under a pile of back numbers of *Forum* and *Men Only* that, with a plastic Thomas the Tank Engine, had been purchased as a job lot, with a Clarice Cliff bowl thrown in, for a tenner. 'They're not quite the sort of old comics and toys we had in mind,' she had explained backing towards the door, when her eye fell on the bowl, holding a dead busy lizzie.

Its owner, a desperate-looking woman hung about with small children, had intercepted her quick appraisal.

'What about the bowl, then? That's antique, it belonged to my grandma.'

'There's no call for that sort of Budgie-Ware,' said Bonnie, her tongue flicking over dry lips, her nose quivering. 'We've got two or three we can't shift, taking up space, gathering dust,' as she flicked the bright feathers of the two birds on a branch of ivy that curved round the pale grey bowl patterned with darker grey leaves.

'They used to give them as prizes at fairgrounds,' Vivien added, lifting the bowl to read the signature on its base. 'They were known as fairings.'

'I thought those were biscuits,' said the woman dully. 'Cornish Fairings?'

14

'Of course, *some* of them *were* biscuits,' Vivien conceded. 'In Cornwall.'

The deal having been struck, the woman was so grateful she made them a cup of pale tea by dunking the same tea bag in two mugs. There were no biscuits. She stroked the birds surreptitiously as she wrapped them in a piece of newspaper. One of the children started to wail 'I don't want those ladies to take our budgies.'

There was the sound of a slap as the door closed. Vivien and Bonnie went whistling to the van.

Six wooden chairs stood in a row in the backyard. Bonnie and Vivien were hard at work in the morning sun, removing the chipped white gloss paint from two of them.

'We'll need some more stripper,' Bonnie said, straightening her back painfully. 'God, how I hate this job.'

'You go and get some and I'll carry on with what's left,' Vivien suggested and Bonnie was only too willing to agree. Fifteen minutes later, satisifed that Bonnie was too far on the road to turn back for anything she might have forgotten, Vivien stripped off the Cornish fisherman's smock she wore for working, pulled on a sweatshirt and, walking as quickly as possible without attracting attention, made for the house.

'This may be the last time I shall come here,' she told it as she stood inside the scullery door, which she left unlocked in case she had to make a quick getaway. The rooks she had startled into raucous proclamation of her guilt lapsed into spasms of complaint in the copper beech. Nobody had rallied to their alarm. Vivien went from room to room, resisting the desire to stroke the dust from satiny fruitwood, walnut, maple, mahogany, to lift the plates from the dresser to read the maker's name, and the marks on the dulling silver in the kitchen, to dust the dead flies from the window ledges and to light the candles in their porcelain sticks. There, on the shelves and in the faded,

15

painted bookcases were all the books she would never read. She longed to take one and curl up in her yellow velvet chair and read the morning away until the yellow dog prevailed upon her to follow him into the garden where a straw hat with lattices broken by time, and a trug awaited her. She admired for the last time the spilled jewels of the crystal doorknob, and stood in front of the glass cabinet committing to memory the figures therein: the man and woman riding on mild goats to meet each other, he with kids' heads peeping from his panniers, and she with hers filled with flowers and a basket of babies on her back, riding homewards in the evening in the cawing of rooks, the . . .

'Is this a private party, or can anybody join in?'

Vivien screamed, whirling round. There, filling the doorway, just like Bea Smith in the latest episode of *Prisoner: Cell Block H*, stood Bonnie, with a knobkerrie in her hand.

'So this is your little game. I've known you were up to something for days.'

'Bea – Bonnie, I can explain.'

'You'd better. You've got a lot of explaining to do – my God, are those what I think they are?'

She advanced on the cabinet.

'Don't touch!'

'Why not? You must've left your dabs all over every-thing. So this is what you were up to. Planned to sell the stuff behind my back and make yourself a juicy little profit, didn't you?'

Bonnie slumped into the yellow chair. 'You were going to leave me, weren't you? Run off and set up on your own.'

Her words were thick and bitter like the tears which rolled from her eyes.

'I'll kill you first.' She leaped up, brandishing the knobkerrie.

'How can you think, I don't believe I'm hearing this – '

16

Vivien caught her raised arm, they fought for the weapon, Bonnie trying frantically to bring it down on Vivien's head, Vivien struggling to hold the murderous arm aloft. A kick in the shins brought howling Bonnie to her knees and Vivien dragged the knobkerrie from her hand. Vivien twisted one of her arms behind her back and pushed her face downwards to the carpet.

'Babe, I love you,' she explained, punctuating her words with light blows from the knobkerrie. 'I swear I wasn't planning to run out on you. I haven't touched anything here, and I'm not going to. Understand?'

'Ouch, you bitch, get off me.' Bonnie spat out carpet fibres.

'If I let you get up, do you promise to sit quietly and listen?'

'Ouch. Thuk.' She spat.

'Very well. Go and sit over there.'

Bonnie slunk, snarling like a dog, to the sofa at which her master pointed the club. A resurgence of rage brought her half to her feet.

'Sit!'

Vivien could see, even after ten minutes of explanation, that Bonnie would never quite believe her. 'It was like being under a spell. As if I was meant to be here. It's so beautiful. So peaceful. I just wanted to be here. It was like being in another world for a little while.'

'Another world from which you excluded me.'

'I was going to tell you. I was going to bring you here later today. I swear.'

'A likely story. Are you sure there's no one else involved? You've been meeting someone here haven't you? Where is she, hiding under the bed? Or is it a he?'

'Don't be so bloody stupid! Look, I'll show you all over the house, you can look under every bed if you like. Can't you get it into your thick skull that I just liked being alone here?'

'No I can't. I never want to be alone without you. I just don't believe you.'

Vivien led Bonnie from room to room. They found no brawny limbs in fluorescent shorts under the beds – nothing but dust, a pair of silver shoes and hanks of horsehair from a torn mattress. Dresses and suits hung empty in the cupboards, linen lay innocently in chests and clean towels were in the airing cupboard, if the spiders in the baths should want them. They pulled their sleeves over their hands to touch knobs and handles. In a chest of drawers they found dozens of kid gloves with pearl buttons never unfastened, in a mille-feuille of virginal tissue paper.

'Satisfied?' They were back in the drawing room. 'Bonnie?'

Bonnie was standing in the centre of the room with a rapt expression on her face.

'Bonnie? It's getting to you, isn't it? The magic of the place. You understand now?'

'What I simply cannot understand, or believe, is how someone who had been in the business as long as you have could be so incredibly stupid as to let such a opportunity pass.'

'You don't understand at all ... I hoped. Oh forget it. Let's go.'

'How could you be so *selfish*? Not telling me. Those wonderful pieces. Just sitting there. Shows how much you value our relationship.'

'It's not like that ...'

'Isn't it?'

'No it isn't.'

Vivien knew she could not defend herself against the charge of wanting to keep the house a secret, or wanting to be alone there. She did not know if that, or her lack of professional loyalty or acumen, was the more hurtful.

'Anyway,' she said, 'this is the last time I'll be coming here. The house goes up for auction next week.'

'Does it? That doesn't give us much time then.'

'No, Bonnie. We're not taking anything.'

Vivien looked from the miniatures and figurines to Bonnie, tear-stained and tense as a whippet, poised on the edge of their marriage.

'Come on then,' she said.

They raced for the stairs. They plundered the glove drawer, forcing their fingers into the unstretched kid; a pearl button hit the floor and rolled away.

'There's a pile of plastic carriers in the kitchen. Where's the van?'

'At home. I watched you leave the house, parked the van and followed you on foot.'

'Good. Thank goodness you didn't bring it here. I should have realised someone was there when the rooks started squawking,' Vivien panted as they worked, each knowing instictively what to take. A team. Although Bonnie would need kid-glove treatment for a while.

'How did you find the key?'

'A toad showed me the way.'

'A toad? Sure you don't mean a robin, like in *The Secret Garden*? I know how you love poring over those mildewed kids' books.'

As Bonnie spoke she jiggled a hairpin, found in a dressing-table tray, in the lock of a china cabinet.

'Brilliant,' Vivien said but she walked over to the window and looked out into the garden as Bonnie lifted out the first cupid and the pretty spotted leopard with gold-tipped paws. They left no mess, no trace of their presence. Vivien locked the door and replaced the wiped key under the plant. As they passed the drawing-room windows she saw the person she might have been, watching them go from the velvet yellow chair in the room defiled by their fight.

They met nobody on the way home but if they had it would have been apparent that those two weirdos from the Old Post Office had been doing their shopping, and not stinting themselves from the look of their bulging bags.

At home Vivien said, 'We must be mad. We'll be the obvious suspects when the stuff's missed. The only dealers for miles around . . . We could put it back . . .'

'And risk getting caught in the act, apart from the fact that this is the biggest coup of our career? No way, José. By the way, how did you know the house is going up for auction?'

'It was in the local paper.'

'Oh. Well, the plan is, we'll drive up to London first thing tomorrow. We can stay with Frankie and Flossie for a few days while we unload the stuff. And I think I know somebody who will be *very* interested . . .'

'But . . .'

'Those frigging freeloaders owe us. Think of the times they've pitched up here without so much as a bottle of Sainsbury's plonk. Besides, they're our best friends!'

The kid gloves shrivelled and blackened on the barbie, giving a peculiar taste to the burgers and green peppers that sweated and spat on the grid above them. The tiny pearl buttons glimmered among the discs of bone, horn, glass and plastic in the tall jar of assorted buttons.

'Shampoo?'

'Shampoo!'

Bonnie and Vivien had returned in high spirits from their successful stay in London. They had taken in a sale of the stock of a bankrupt theatrical costumiers on the way back. It was nine o'clock in the evening. The man on the doorstep heard music and caught a glimpse of two figures, beyond the nude in her hat and necklace, locked together in a slow dance once known as the Gateways grind, out of sync with the jaunty song.

20

'Good evening, ladies. Filth,' he smiled, flashing his ID at the wolf in a lime-green beaded dress who answered the door.

'Who is it?' came the bark of the fox just behind her.

'It's the Filth – I mean the police,' came the slightly muffled reply. For a moment they stood, the wolf in green and the fox in a scarlet sheath fringed with black, staring at him with glassy eyes, then simultaneously pulled off their heads, and he felt that they had removed their sharp, sly masks to reveal features identical to the heads they held in their hands, so that he still faced a fox and wolf, but with fear in their eyes.

He touched delicately one of the tubular beads on Bonnie's dress, standing in his linen suit crumpled from a day's policing. 'Nice,' he said. 'Bugle beads, aren't they? That's Blossom Dearie, isn't it?' He sang *There ought to be a moonlight-saving time, so I could love that man of mine . . .* glancing towards the uniformed constable at the wheel of the police car.

'You'd better come in,' said Vivien the Fox. The animals, on high heels, led them into the front room. He saw a bottle of champagne and two glasses.

'I don't suppose you'd like a drink? You can't when you're on duty, can you?'

'You've been watching too much television,' he replied, picking up a dusty green glass from a sideboard. 'Regular Aladdin's cave you've here, haven't you? Cheers.' He raised his glass to the model and looked round at the piles and rails of clothes, the jumble of china and glass, silver, brass and pewter, the old books, the trivia, the ephemera that refused to die, the worthless and the valuable bits of furniture, the glass jar that held the tiny pearl buttons snipped from two pairs of burned skin gloves.

'I caught one of her shows at the Pizza on the Park,' he said. 'Blossom Dearie.'

'Oh, so did we!' Vivien exclaimed, 'Perhaps – '

'How can we help you?' Bonnie broke in.

'There's been a break-in. At an empty house down the road, the old Emerson place. Some valuable pieces taken. I've got the list here. We thought you might come across some of them in your travels, or someone might try to pass them off on you, you being the most local and obvious outlet – if our perpetrators are the bunch of amateurs we suspect they are. If that should happen, we'd be very grateful if you would let us know.'

'Of course.' Vivien took the photocopied list he held out. It shook in her hand although there was no draught that humid evening.

'Let's see.' Bonnie read aloud over Vivien's shoulder. 'Meissen Shepherdess with birdcage. Harlequin and Columbine, cupids representing four seasons. Leopard. Man and woman, riding goats, Staffordshire. Chelsea, Derby, Bow . . . pair of berry spoons, circa 1820 . . .'

She whistled. 'There's some nice stuff here. Priceless. Any idea who could have done the job?'

'We're working on it. Whoever it was did a pretty good demolition job on the drawing room and kindly left us a few genetic fingerprints. Shouldn't be too difficult.'

The fox went as red as the cherries on the dummy's hat, as if she had been responsible for the violation.

'But those lovely things – the shepherdess, the leopard, the porcelain – what were they doing in an empty house? Wasn't there a burglar alarm at least to protect them?'

'The house and contents were due to be auctioned the following day. It was just bad luck. Old Mrs Emerson's godson, she left it to him, has no interest in the place apart from the proceedings from the sale – serves him right, really. Nasty piece of work – greedy and careless – a dangerous combination. More money than sense already. There's an old local couple who kept an eye on the place – he did a bit in the garden, kept the grass down, and she kept the dust down. It seems likely that one of them forgot to reset the alarm the last time they were there, but that's academic really. They're both in deep shock. Aged ten years overnight. Heartbroken. Keep saying they've betrayed old Mrs Emerson's trust. From the look of them they'll be apologising to her in person soon ... Well, thank you for your co-operation. Sorry to intrude on your evening.'

'We were just pricing some new stock,' Bonnie felt obliged to explain, waving a hand at the fox and wolf heads staring at them from the floor, as he rose to leave.

'Phew!! What an incredible stroke of luck! That someone should actually break in while we were away! I can't believe it! Somebody up there must like us ...' Bonnie sank into a chair kicking off her high-heeled shoes.

'And us prancing around like a couple of drag queens in animal heads,' she went on, 'I thought I would die. I could hear those prison gates clanging, couldn't you! Cell Block H, here we come! Let's have a look at that list again. "Silver salt spoon, convolvulus design handle"? How come we missed that?'

'I don't know.'

Vivien crossed her fingers behind her back and hoped that Tedina, who had watched her unscrew the brass knob of the bedpost and drop in a silver spoon, would keep her mouth shut. Then the spoon with its convolvulus wreathed stem would lie safely and inaccessibly locked in the bedpost, a tiny silver secret salvaged from her house, as long as the marriage lasted. She pulled the chenille bedspread that served as a curtain across the window, refilled their glasses and turned over the record.

'Where were we, before we were so rudely interrupted?

She held out both her hands and they resumed the dance; the Friendly Old-Established Firm, back in business.

Angelo

The long brown beans in the catalpa rattled in the wind, brittle pods dangling in bunches among the last flapping yellow leaves of the tree, so ancient and gnarled that it rested on a crutch, in the courtyard of St James's, Piccadilly. Splintered pods and big damp leaves littering the stones were slippery under the feet of the friends, enemies and those who wished to be seen at Felix Mazzotti's Memorial Service. Drizzle gave a pearly lustre to black umbrellas and brought up the velvet pelts of collars, and cashmere and cloth, moistened hats and vivified patterned shawls and scarves.

Violet Greene settled herself and her umbrella in a pew beside a stranger. The umbrella's handle was an ivory elephant's head, yellow and polished by time like a long old tooth, the grooves in its trunk smoothed by generations of gloves. The heavy white paper of the Order of Service in her black velvet fingers, thick gold-leaf braid trimming white stone, glittering brass; Violet concentrated on these, and caught the little black eye of the elephant's head, which *was* an old tooth, taken from some Victorian tusker too long ago to worry about, and carved into little replicas of its original owner. Round her neck Violet wore a string of jet beads, mourning jewellery which Felix had given her forty years before. Felix's mother had been English, his father Italian, and although he was officially a Catholic he had never felt the slightest twitch on the thread. Hence this church rather than the Brompton Oratory or Farm Street. The lapse of time between the news of his death, and the funeral which had been a private affair in Italy, and the memorial service had accustomed people to his absence from the world, and time in any case rushes in as the sea fills holes in the sand.

When someone is shot, Violet had read, they often feel no pain at first; she had waited, after the bullet's impact of the news, for the wound of loss to bleed and burn, but she had not seen Felix for five years – which was good because she had no picture of him as the really old man he had suddenly become – although they had spoken occasionally on the telephone and it was hard to remember that he was dead. One day she had decided to believe that he was still in his terraced garden among the olive trees that gave the beautiful green oil of which he was so proud, and felt a release. It was so simple she wondered why she had not thought of it sooner. He had once told her that his olive oil gave him more pleasure and sense of achievement than all the books he had written. It had seemed such an arrogant remark, one that could have been made only by somebody as successful in the world's eye as he was, that she had felt irritated for days. Even though she refused to recognise his death, questions would persist: What were we like? What were we like together? Who was I then? She had been sixteen when they met, he a much older man of thirty. A mere boy. And was that girl herself, Violet Clements, in a silky dress printed with pansies under a cheap, black cloth coat shivering in the March wind on the steps of a house in Gordon Square? On her way to the church in a taxi this morning she had passed a bed of blue and yellow pansies, and watched the colours quivering, trembling with the taxi's motor, the dyes running together in the rivulets on the wet glass.

Her black velvet beret with its soft pleats like the gills of a large field mushroom was skewered with a black

25

pearl clasped in two tiny silver hands, and she wore an emerald scarf of fine wool in a loose triangle across the shoulders of her black coat. Violet Greene she was now, and supposed that Greene, her fourth surname, would be her last, although she would not quite have put money on it. She rather liked it; the pre-Raphaelite purple and viridian of her name, the hectic hues of Arthur Hughes, or of bright green Devon Violets scent in a round bottle with painted flowers. Or Cornish, Welsh, Scottish or Parma violets – the cachou odour was the same, and a sniff of it would recall seaside holidays with the boys, salt-caked plimsolls and rough sandy towels bleaching on the rail of a wooden veranda. A present for the best mother in the world brought with pennies saved out of their ice-cream money. Today a delicate waft of toilet-water was all but indiscernible as she moved.

The organ was playing a medley, a melancholy fruit cocktail in heavy syrup, as the pews filled. Violet was clasping her hands, not in prayer but to restrain them from plucking a silver hair from the coat in front of her, when a finger prodded her own back. She turned.

'Hello. I like your hat. Is it what's called a Van Dyck beret?'

Violet had made a decision long ago not to dislike a girl simply because she was young and beautiful, so she smiled at the whisperer under her hooded eyes, still violet but faded, as the flowers do. Someone's daughter or granddaughter, some child in publishing or from a gallery, in PR, met at some party – she was still invited to more than she bothered with; a fixture on some guestlists after so many years on the sidelines of the arts. She couldn't remember. All black lycra and red lipstick, with long fair hair that required to be raked back from her face every few seconds; the sort of girl seen at the cinema with a giant bucket of popcorn, climbing over people's legs, drawing attention to herself.

26

'It's my first time at one of these,' the girl confided in her loud whisper. 'I s'pose you must've been to hundreds . . .'

'Thousands,' Violet confirmed drily.

The girl's hat lying on the pew was the kind of crushed velvet thing you would see on a stall at Camden Market between racks of discarded dresses that might have belonged to Violet long ago and she had evidently lost confidence in her ability to wear it. Violet never went out without a hat, linen and straw with a rose or cherries or a floating scarf; canvas, wool or feline print; she was known for her amusing and assured headgear in a time when so few women knew how. Her ear picked up a few bars of 'What'll I do' interwoven plaintively through strands of 'Sheep May Safely Graze', 'Voi Che Sapete', 'Memories' and 'For All We Know' . . . *For all we know, this may only be a dream. We come and go like ripples on a stream. Time like an ever rolling stream bears all its sons away. They fly forgotten as a dream. . . . Imagine there's no heaven* . . . she was aware of the girl behind her slewing round in her pew, and the velvet hat was proving useful, she saw as she turned her head a fraction, waving frantically at some young people hesitating noisily at the back of the church, flapping them into the seats bagged for them. They should have been holding enormous paper cups of Coca-Cola rattling with ice-cubes, and straws to hoover it up, rather than those unfamiliar prayer books with which they had been issued.

Here we are, out of cigarettes . . . two sleepy people by dawn's early light, too much in love to say good-night . . . Who had chosen this music? Felix's third wife, the charmless Camilla, over there in the Liberty hair band, in the first flush of middle-age but still young enough to be his granddaughter, with children from her first marriage, who took none of his references, responded to his jokes with serious replies, mirthless barks or groans, didn't smoke, and bridled at the mention of Violet's name. There were bits of bridle or snaffles or some piece of harness across her shoes, vestiges of the nurse she had become to Felix clung to her as if demanding respect for an invisible uniform of self-sacrifice. It was hideous to imagine her snouting through naive old letters, selecting the worst photographs of Violet for the authorised biography. The only redress would be to write her own memoirs, but Violet lacked the energy or inclination to do it, and although she had given up poetry many years ago, she remembered the torture of trying to recreate the truth in words, even when only trying to describe a landscape or a lampshade.

Her uncharitable thoughts about Camilla were prompted by Camilla's hostility to her, concealed today for appearance's sake. She resented being cast as a witch, an *old* witch, because Felix had loved her best. Violet Clements had been orphaned at fourteen and a year later had left her aunt's crowded house to make her own way in the world. She had got a job at a small printing press whose decorative hand-blocked volumes were collectors' items now, and at night she had filled notebooks with her own verses by the gaslight of her attic room. She had met Felix at a tea party given by one of their poets, where absinthe was offered in rose-painted cups. The poet, killed in the war and his work forgotten, had called for a toast to 'the green fairy' as he poured the romantic liquid. Violet took only a sip or two of infamous anise but she was under the green fairy's spell, in love with and in awe of the shabby glamour of the bad fairy's court.

Felix's invitation to coffee to show him her poems filled her with joy and terror for he was an established novelist and man of letters and so she was trembling with awe as much as from the March wind when she rang his bell. Shocked, for Felix wore a spotted dressing-gown, she backed down the steps blushing and starting to apologise, not looking at his bare legs, thinking she had got the wrong day. He laughed. He lead her into a room with an unmade bed.

'But it's the morning!'

He had laughed again.

The poems in her bag, so carefully selected, wilted like wallflowers at a party. It was cold, painful, and above all excruciatingly embarrassing. Violet's face had blazed for hours like the gas-fire he lit afterwards, and drinking the black bitter coffee which he had made at last, she could neither look at him nor speak.

'Violet Greene has a string of lovers,' she overheard somebody say years later, and she saw herself on Primrose Hill, against a yellow sky, pulled across the horizon by the pack of dogs whose leashes cut into her hand. Four of her former lovers were in the church today, she counted, and Felix, if she were to admit to it, was scattered over the grass at Kenwood where leafless autumn crocuses shivered on their white stalks like girls gone mauve with the cold. Camilla had brought his ashes to England in a casket.

'Who would true valour see
Let him come hither;
One here will constant be,
Come wind, come weather;

'There's no discouragement
Shall make him once relent
His first avowed intent
To be a pilgrim.'

Violet's eyes blurred, and she had to control her mouth which was unable to do more than mime the words. From Kensington nursing home and Oxford, Sutton Scotney, Bloomsbury, Maida Vale, Hampstead and points south

29

the pilgrims had come this wild morning, old playmates summoned by the cracked bell of Fitzrovia.

'Bloody Brighton train!'

Maurice Wolverson edged into the pew beside her, knocking her umbrella to the floor, in a fury about leaves on the line. 'Not a bad house,' he commented, looking around.

Mingled smells of damp wool and linseed oil came off the camel-hair coat whose velvet lapels were stippled with flake-white, and then an amber peaty aroma rose as he unscrewed the silver top of his cane. He drew out a long glass tube and offered it to Violet, who shook her head. His last part, four years ago, had been a walk-on in a television sit-com set in a seaside home for retired thespians. He had taken to daubing views of Brighton's piers to block out the sound of the swishing tide while waiting for the telephone to ring. A cluster of tarry shingle was stuck to the sole of his shoe and a red and white spotted handkerchief in his pocket made a crumpled attempt at jauntiness.

'They'll have to paper the house when my turn comes,' Maurice muttered. Violet patted his knee.

'Choirboys. On a scale of one to ten . . .?'

Violet slapped his knee.

Looking back she was incredulous, and indignant on the behalf of all foolish young women who took themselves at a man's valuation, that her fear and distaste had been compounded by worry that her body might not meet Felix's high standards, for he and his circle were harsh arbiters of female pulchritude. She had been half afraid that the jaded gourmet might send back the roast spring lamb.

'Well, what did you expect?' he had asked, 'turning up on my doorstep looking like that?'

Apologies had come years later. Even now, Violet knew that she brightened in men's company, became prettier,

30

wittier, revived like a thirsty flower, with a silver charge through her veins. She had never succumbed to sensible underwear or footwear and no giveaway little pickled-onion bulge distorted her shoes.

Her eyes closed as she listened to the anthem, and she felt a pang of affection for Felix's olive oil, and let the viscous yellow-green drip slowly from the bottle with the label he had designed, until it brimmed on the spoon, sharing his pleasure in it, not arguing. She had hated him often as he pursued her down the years like Dracula in an opera cloak or a degenerate Hound of Heaven, and she had carried a bagful of grievances against him about with her, but now the drawstrings of the bag loosened and all the old withered hurts, wrongs and frustrations flew out and upwards to the rafters, unravelled and dissolved in the gold and amber voices of the choir. As they knelt to pray, she ran the jet beads through her hand like a rosary, feeling the facets through the fingers of her gloves.

A nudge in the ribs jolted her. 'Was it Beverley Nichols or Godfrey Winn who had a dog called Mr Sponge?' came in a stage whisper.

Violet squeezed her eyes shut tight: 'Oh God, please bless Felix and let him be happy and reunited with his family and – ' If there were a heaven, it was a good thing for her and most of this congregation that there was no marriage or giving in marriage there. Imagine the complications.

'Which of them got Willie Maugham's desk in the end?'

'Oh God, *I* don't know.' She didn't know, didn't know if her prayer would get through the myriad, innumerable as plankton, prayers eternally sluicing the teeth of heaven's gate. A snowball's chance in hell perhaps. 'Ask them yourself – later!' Her words hissed like sizzling snow.

*

A teenage boy, perhaps one of Camilla's, was standing at the front of the church, clearing his throat. He read badly, as if he had never read any poetry until this public occasion; it was Francis Thompson's 'At Lord's' that the boy was murdering but could not quite kill. Violet's eyes filled again, and her unshed tears were brackish with bitterness. The poem had brought her back to Felix once when she had been on the point of leaving him. They were in a taxi, his coat was speckled with ash and she had recoiled from his tobacco-stained kiss. They must have been passing Lord's for she had mentioned the poem, that she thought was her own discovery, a manly poem that had touched her girl's heart, and Felix had at once recited it, word perfect, and she had felt an overwhelming tenderness for him. How dared Camilla know about it? He had spread himself thin like rich pâté eked out over too many slices of toast. Desolate, small and old, she would have given almost anything to be riding in that taxi through the blue London twilight now. But Felix was in Italy, she braced up, pontificating over a bottle of young wine or extra virgin oil, holding it up to the light.

She forbade the tears to spill, it would not do for people to see her – unmanned. A man's woman – yes, she had always been that. Her women friends had always taken second place to the man in her life. 'Flies round a honeypot,' Felix would snort with jealous pride after every party. Had the essence of herself been dissipated, though, and nearly all her choices made for her, by some man's or boy's need which outweighed her own?

At a splash to her right, she glanced at Maurice. Tears were rolling down his cheeks and dripping on to his Order of Service. She gave a sharp nod at the handkerchief in his top pocket. Upstaged. She swallowed an untimely giggle that threatened to turn into a sob.

As Denzil, Sir Denzil Allen, ancient ousted publisher, began his address, Violet thought, this is odd. Very odd, if you come to think of it, as she did. She referred to her Order of Service to confirm her suspicion: all the speakers and readers were men. Felix had been such a lover of women, many of his closest friends had been women and yet those women he had loved and who had known him best, herself chief among them, were to sit in their pews and have him expounded to them by these men. Well, that was the way of the world which she had made no attempt to change, and she could have been Violet Mazzotti and have organised this service herself, and made a better job of it. Women had not always been nice to her. She remembered the resentment, the thinly veiled spite of some of Felix's old friends when they were living together. Men too. Had she really expected them to say, 'Welcome, Violet Clements, lovely and gifted youthful poet. We embrace you as one of us'? She could understand them now, but she had often been hurt and she stuck to her resolve never to snub a young girl, however pretty or silly, in whom shyness might be mistaken for arrogance.

Across the church she could see Sibyl Warner, the novelist, making a rare appearance. Heavily veiled, once a great beauty, she had long been a recluse from a world which assumed the right to comment on time's alterations. 'My God, I didn't recognise you! You've changed!' That wound inflicted twenty years ago by Jill Blakiston, in an affronted tone which hinted at betrayal and that the photographs on the jackets of Sibyl's books must have been forgeries. Jill sat behind Violet today, a retired editorial director, rummaging in a £1000 worth of crocodile bag, quite unaware of what she had done, but Violet had been there and seen Sibyl flinch and gulp her drink in her eagerness to leave.

Something had shocked Violet almost as much as the revelation that people could go to bed in the morning. 'Mind if I pee in your sink?' Felix had asked. It was a year

33

after they had met and she was living in a respectable boarding house in Mornington Crescent. She most certainly had minded. There was her cake of carnation soap on the rim of the basin and her sponge and toothbrush in a glass. 'This is intolerable,' Felix had said. 'The sooner you move in with me the better.'

Her landlady, catching Felix tiptoeing down the stairs at one in the morning, told her to pack her bags at once and so, in a cloud of disgrace and defiance, she departed to Gordon Square. Living in sin entailed, she found out, a great deal of scrubbing shirt collars and darning socks and hours of copying out manuscripts and typing. But it had been fun too. Fun – what a funny, bizarre, orange paper-hat word. After a while afternoon drinking clubs and hangovers and cooking for Felix's drunken friends wasn't fun any more. Felix sailed to America in 1938, for which some still condemned him. Violet had refused to accompany him and when he returned she was Violet Morton, a widow with two children, the younger boy born posthumously after the Battle of Britain. Violet had married George Maxwell-Smith to give the boys a father, and divorced him after he had gambled away his father's furniture factory and fled with the girl in accounts. Her third husband, Bobby Greene, a painter, had succumbed to cancer after just eighteen months of happy marriage. His pictures hung on her walls and there had been intimations recently of a small renaissance of interest in his work.

> 'Hold Thou Thy Cross
> Before my closing eyes.
> Shine through the gloom
> And point me to the skies . . .'

An amethyst cross, grown huge, loomed gleaming through swirling mist, suspended above Felix's bed; Felix rising vertically ceilingward with feet pointed down. An amethyst cross on a silver chain that had belonged to her mother, pawned and never redeemed.

As always after one of these occasions Violet was left with the thought that all that really matters in this life is that we should be kind to one another.

'Imogen, there's no heaven!' she heard a boy say outside, under the Indian bean tree leaning on its crutch.

'Ha ha, very funny,' said Imogen, the girl who had been behind Violet, and blew her nose, saying, 'Has my mascara run all over the place? You know, I really quite enjoyed that.'

A group of black-coated youngish Turks was lighting cigarettes, and one of them cast a satirical eye at the knot of Violet's friends moving towards her, and made a remark at which the others laughed. Violet wondered when the power had passed to those young men with sliding smiles and snidey eyes; when had they staged their coup? She glanced around and thought: you – girl in a black dress squirming away from the poet you had thought to flatter with your charm – you have read none of his work but someone told you he is a poppet, and now he's threatening your cleavage with the dottle from his pipe. Who are all these rouged dotards, you wonder, boys and girls, these deposed old Turks who sidle up to you with swimming eyes like macerated cocktail cherries pleading for a reissue of their mildewed masterworks, a mention on the wireless, or a book to review that you will never send? Who are they, these mothballed revenant that you thought dead for years, these relics of whom you have never heard. Who? Well, my dears – they are you.

Violet was weary: wake up, Denton Welch, Djuna Barnes, Mark Gertler, Gaudier-Brzeska, Gjurdieff, et al – it's time for your next brief disinterment. Angels were warming up to dance on the heads of pins. A bored miaow

35

from Schroeder's Cat. Stale buns, duckies. It was reassuring to be kissed by old kid and chamois leather, badger bristle shaving-brushes and paintbrush beards, comfortable if elegaic to be surrounded by elegant decaying warehouses that had stored fine wines and cheeses and garlic for most of the century, some who were as stout as their sodden purple-seeping vats and others as frail as towers of round plywood boxes that might topple and be bowled along by the wind.

'Are you coming along for drinkies?'

'No, Maurice dear, my grandson's taking me out to lunch.'

He was, but on the following day. Violet had had enough. It had been gracious of Camilla to invite her today, perhaps, but enough was enough. She disengaged herself and started to walk towards Fortnum's, rather worried about Maurice. Who would pour him into the Brighton train in the frightful gloaming when the lights of shops and taxis blaze bleakly on wan faces and all souls seem lost? Would some sixth sense carry him along, a buffeted buffoonish bygone, with the cruel and censorious commuters, or might he find himself alone on the concourse but for a few vagrants, Lily Law bearing down on him, the last train gone and all bars closed, or would he wake without a passport at Gatwick Airport, or in a black siding at Hassocks or Haywards Heath? She consoled herself with the knowledge that it was the drinks afterwards which had persuaded him to make the journey to the service, and that after a certain hour everybody on the Brighton train was drunk. Deciding against Fortnum's, she turned down Duke Street into Jermyn Street, making for St James's Square. The shop windows were lovely, still dressed for autumn with coloured leaves and berries, nuts and gilded rosy pomegranates, but behind the glass of one display an aerosol forecast snow.

*

Violet loved the symmetry of the gardens, that square within a circle within a square within a square. She sat on a bench with a sense of being alone with the equestrian statue of Guilelmus III at its centre and the birds that fluttered in the foliage and pecked about in the fallen leaves on the paving stones. An obelisk marked each corner of the inner square, a tiny leaved rambling rose had captured one of them and held it in its thorns, and a wren emerged from a bush, saw her and disappeared. Her eyes were still sharp enough to identify a bird; she was fortunate in that. She was fortunate in having a tall, fair-haired grandson. Had there been a touch of smugness in her tone when she had spoken of him to poor lonely Maurice? Well, she *was* proud of Tom and delighted that he should want to take her to lunch; too bad, why should she temper her feelings to Maurice's sensibilities? She did try not to condescend to those who were not the mother of sons and had only grand-daughters, instead of big handsome boys who made one feel cherished and feminine and even a little deliciously dotty and roguish at times, and it was pleasant to bring out carefully selected stories from her past as if from a drawer lined with rose and violet pot-pourri spiced with faint intriguing muskier fruitier notes. Maurice had been involved in some unpleasantness in the bad old days, she recalled, but he must have put aside all such foolishness now, as she had. The long windows of the London Library glittered, reminding her how once she would have hoped love lurked there, playing peek-a-boo round the book stacks. She toyed with the idea of a cup of coffee in the Wren, the wholesome café attached to the church, or something worthy to eat, but putting that aside in favour of her own little kitchen and bathroom, along with the unpleasant image, like a grey illustration in a book, of Maurice in a suit of broad arrows breaking stones in Reading Gaol, she decided to take the Piccadilly line to Gloucester Road.

*

There wasn't a seat and Violet had to stand, but just for a moment or two until a rough-looking lad heaved himself up and nodded her into his place. Violet thanked him courteously, giving a lesson in manners to any who should be watching, and a rueful, apologetic little smile to the dowdy woman left standing. It doesn't do to judge by appearances, she thought, of the boy, while acknowledging that he, naturally, had done just that. It didn't surprise her because it had always been so; men had never stopped holding doors open for her, and even when she and the boys had been marooned in that rotting thatched cottage in Suffolk after George's defection, there had been some gum-booted Galahad to dig her out of a ditch or rescue a bird from the chimney.

A startlingly beautiful boy was sitting opposite her. She couldn't take her eyes off his face. About sixteen, with loose blue-black curls, olive skin and a full, tragic mouth. He must be South American. Venezuelan, she decided, in a city far from home. He had the face of an angel. She named him Angelo. There was a panache, a muted stylishness, about his black leather jacket, dark charcoal sweater over a white T-shirt, black jeans, silver ring and earring, the black-booted ankle resting casually across the knee. Fearing that he might imagine there was something predatory in the way she drank in his beauty, she averted her attention to the ill-featured youth on Angelo's right, but she was drawn back to Angelo's almond-shaped, lustrous, long-lashed eyes. Hyde Park Corner came and went. Violet shut her eyes, abruptly suffused by a sadness she didn't know what to do with, and a statue came into her mind, a little stone saint in a wayside shrine whose lips had crumbled, kissed away by thousands of supplicants' desires. She wanted to warn the boy: Angelo, beware. People will prey on you, want to possess you, corrupt you, exploit you for your beauty until there is nothing left of you and you are destroyed; but

38

there was a wariness about Angelo's face which said that he had learned that long ago.

She opened her eyes. A sudden instinct told her that Angelo and the youth who had given up his seat and the lout on his right were connected, and pretending not to be. A lunge of silver, her bag ripped from her hands, fingers tearing at her rings, and as he grabbed the necklace, black against a blazing yellow and grape-purple flash of anguished desire to snatch back and relive her years, she was aware of a knife at her throat and that Angelo was a girl.

A Mine of Serpents

Gerald found two burnt-out rockets in the front garden when he went to check that the dustmen had replaced the lids properly. Bonfire night went on for weeks nowadays, it seemed, with bangs like gunshots ricocheting off the pavements and fracturing the sky. Some of them probably were gunshots. Two of his tenants, Kathy and her little boy Stefan, came down the steps, going to school.

'Got all your fireworks for tonight, then?' Gerald accosted the boy, 'All your bangers and rockets, eh?'

'No, they're too dangerous. We're going to the organised display at Crystal Palace.'

'Too dangerous?! Organised display?! We used to *burn down* Crystal Palace every Guy Fawkes when *I* was a nipper!' Gerald was gratified by the kid's doubtful look at his mother.

'No, of course not,' she snapped. 'Mr Creedy was teasing you.'

'Why?' he heard as Stefan trotted along, skinny as a sparkler with his little plastic lunchbox, the wind billowing out his pink and green jacket like a spinnaker, or an air balloon that might take flight and drift over the rooftops. No such luck.

'Catherine wheels,' he shouted after them. 'Named for your mum. Saint Catherine!'

Kathy, with a K, hunched her shoulders in her thin jacket. Pleased with the history lessons he had given the

40

child, Gerald disinfected the bins. His description of his young self as a nipper was apt: he and his twin Harold had been nippy as corgis, in their hand-knit cardigans; biting the legs of other children, up to sly dodges, smirking, ears pricked, Brylcreemed quiffs a-quiver as the cane swished innocent flinching flesh. The Creedy twins were not popular but their dyadic aspect gave them status; two-faced, double-dealing, duplicitous, two peas in a pod, they needed no one else. Maggoty peas, some said.

Now Gerald uprooted a painful thought of Harold, with a green weed that had dared to survive the first frost and flaunt itself from the drain. Harold, estranged and sulking, six doors away. No weeds were permitted on board *Bromley Villa*; Gerald ran a tight ship; if he didn't care for the cut of your jib . . . similarly, all was shipshape and Bristol fashion at *Bickley*, Harold's trim craft – the nautical analogies stop here; the twins had been drummed out of the Second South Norwood Sea Scouts, dismissed the Service with dishonour after several shipmates had walked the plank off the coast of Bognor. Gerald's enquiry of little Stefan about fireworks had been routine malice; not so much as a damp squib would be allowed to violate the back lawn of *Bromley*, or, God forbid, fire to flicker anywhere near the garden shed.

On his way upstairs, Gerald passed the half-open door of Madame Alphonsine and glimpsed her laying out the Tarot. She waved a card in greeting; the Hanged Man as usual, he supposed. What a disaster her tenancy was, and yet he had been powerless to prevent it, putty, or molten wax, in her pudgy, baubled hand. One day a leaflet had come through his door, advising of her psychic expertise in palmistry and with the crystal ball. It gave, unaccountably, his address. The next day she had materialised and somehow become ensconced, with her scented candles and other noxious paraphernalia, in the vacant room which he had not yet advertised, and since then loonies had

41

trooped in to have their gullible palms read and cross hers with silver, in addition to the folding money she charged for solving Problems of Love, Health and Finance, and casting out Evil Spirits. One confused supplicant had brought a sickly potted palm.

Gerald had sought the help of the Church to cast Madame Alphonsine out. Father O'Flynn, sitting in the Presbytery sucking broth through a straw, for a parishioner had socked him in the jaw, shook his head sadly. The Reverend Olwyn of Belvedere Road Reformed played him a tape of Doris Day singing 'Que Sera Sera'.

'Ours is a Broad Church, Duckie . . .' She told him, striking a match on her cassock.

'Necessarily,' he replied, squeezing past her.

Tony, from Some Saints, popped round at Gerald's request and got a promise from Alphonsine to drop in at next Sunday's Wine and Bread Do, and some items for the Operation Steeplechaser Car Boot, most of them highly unsuitable; and Mr Dearborn of The True Light of Beulah embraced her with a hearty 'Praise the Lord! Sister Alphonsine! Long time no see!'

'Yo, Reverend,' said Madame Alphonsine.

Gerald had given up.

Madame Alphonsine heard his master-key in the locks of the tenants who were out, and his footsteps going downstairs. She had heard, too, his conversation with Stefan. From her window she watched old Miseryguts pottering about in the garden, shaking his fist at a mocking splash of pink stars against the cold blue sky; set off, no doubt, by some kiddies truanting from school, bless them. He had been like a bear with a sore head since his quarrel with his brother. The needle in the wax noddle was working nicely. She saw him unlock his precious shed and disappear inside.

*

Harold would not be the only absentee tonight; Gerald's two friends would be otherwise engaged. They missed the fireworks every year. By November the fifth they were right down at the bottom of their box, as still and cold to the touch as two abandoned ostrich eggs in a nest of straw. Percy and Bysshe were tortoises. As if they had copies of the Church's Calendar in their shells, they would rise again at Easter, symbolising stones rolled away from the tomb, their dusty carapaces patterned like chocolate Easter eggs.

'Why do you call them Percy and Bysshe?' Gerald lived in hope of being asked.

'Because they're Shelley,' he would reply. The old jokes were the best. His had amused Harold for thirty years. To think they had fallen out at their time of life, and over their birthday cake. Each had accused the other of eating a crystallised violet before the candles had been lit. In fact, Gerald had eaten it, but he was damned if he was going to back down now. And neither, of course, would Harold. Well, let him eat cake until it came out of his silly, pointed ears. No, the ears weren't silly; Gerald rubbed his own; rather unusual design, that was all. Distinguished. Having checked that the tortoises' hibernating box was undisturbed, he locked the shed. A piercing pain shot down his leg. He cried out as something sharp stabbed the other leg. It was as if his trousers were peppered with burning shot. He danced from foot to foot, slapping and rubbing at himself. The pains vanished as suddenly as they had attacked, and he was left feeling shaken and foolish, incredulous that his skin was not pitted with tiny wounds.

He sat down in the kitchen, grateful that he *could* sit down, with a cup of tea and a bag of marshmallows. As he dunked, a little smile played over his lips while the faint pins-and-needles in his legs evoked happier Bonfire Nights of long ago: the time he and Harold had filled that girl's gumboots with Jumping Jacks, and didn't *she* jump, with her wellygogs going off like firecrackers. Actually, they hadn't; that had been a cherished fantasy; even the Creedy twins had not been so stupid and cruel; but he recalled the exhilarating smell of gunpowder in the air; waiting for Dad to come home to light the bonfire, rockets in milk bottles, Catherine wheels nailed to the fence, chucking bangers into the fire, cocoa and burning black and cindery roasted spuds, melting marshmallows on sticks, whose bubbles blistered your mouth; the clanging of ambulance bells and fire engines racing along the streets. Oh the glamour of those firework names, Bengal matches, Roman candles, Mount Vesuvius, Silver Rain; the weeks of eyeing them in the corner shop, planning what to get; the thrill of pinching them from under old blind Mrs Hennessey's nose, (the shame of being frog-marched to the police station). But the most prized, the most wonderful of all, had been the Mine of Serpents. Magic and evil, the fat midnight blue cylinder printed with red and yellow waited magnificently until last to explode its writhing gold and crimson snakes into the black sky.

Everything had changed, and for the worse. Homogenised and bland. Only yesterday, in the supermarket, he had seen hot towels like the kind you got in Indian restaurants; to be microwaved for use at garden barbecues. Lost in reverie, he consumed the pink and white pillows: Light the blue touchpaper and retire. Do not hold in the hand. Do not return to a firework once lit; every year somebody had returned to school scarred; one boy had never returned. Gerald ate until he felt like a bloated cushion, overstuffed with pallid foam rubber. The thought of the glorious time a spark from the Creedys' bonfire had ignited next-door's Giant Selection box failed to revive him, and he went to lie down. The pains in his legs started up, his head ached, he had cramps in his arms. If they

44

didn't wear off, he'd have to go to the doctor. If Harold were here, he'd know what to do. He thought about Madame Alphonsine; she had brought trouble on his house. Why had she been guided to Bromley Villa by her crystal ball? He consoled himself with Percy and Bysshe, safe from frost, fire, thieves and predators, snug as two bugs. He wondered miserably if Harold would be eating hot dogs and candyfloss at Crystal Palace, or watching pyrotechnics on the Thames on his black and white telly to the sound of Handel's Firework Music, while Gerald lay dying.

At five o'clock he limped out to the surgery, passing Madame Alphonsine and a client in the hall.

'. . . a long robe?' the client was saying, 'OK, and what did you say he'd be carrying? A scythe? Right, I'll watch out for him. Thanks, see you, then.'

Green vapour trailed in the sky, a crimson chrysanthemum showered its petals as he hobbled against the tide of people heading for Crystal Palace.

'Ten pence for the Guy?' two children begged him.

'Call that a Guy? You ought to be ashamed of yourselves!' Gerald kicked the black plastic sack that formed its body, bursting the balloon that was an apology for a head, and yelled as a burning needle skewered his foot.

He sat in the waiting room reading a poster: Follow the Firework Code. Keep Pets Indoors. His were. The doctor could find nothing wrong with him.

Gerald was feeling much better when he arrived home. The back door was wide open; he couldn't believe it. There was a fire in the middle of the lawn, Stefan was capering round it with a sparkler, like a demented elf with a fizzing wand; they were all out there, all the tenants. Madame Alphonsine was handing round cocoa. But most terrible, terrible, the shed door was swinging open on its hinges. He rushed out. His darlings were gone! Their box was

45

gone. He ran to the fire, to tear it apart with his bare hands.

'Where are they, where are they, what have you done? Murderers! Murderers!' His voice rose in a harsh scream as they held him back.

'Where are who?'

'My tortoises! My boys . . .'

'But you took them yourself! I saw you!' Kathy was shouting. 'In a wheelbarrow!'

Then he saw it all. Only one person would be spiteful enough to take the tortoises. Dear old Harold. With the spare key entrusted to him. The tortoises were safe. He looked across the back gardens. Puffs of smoke were coming from the garden of Bickley. Harold sending smoke signals. Signalling triumph. Ignoring the grinning Guy burning in a suit exactly like his best, Gerald grabbed the heavy blue and red and yellow shawl from Madame Alphonsine's head and flapped it above the flames; signalling a truce under the shooting stars and sea-anemones and serpents that floated in the sky.

Glass

The bus shelter was a skeleton. Her feet crunched its smashed glass, like coarse soda crystals under her shoes as she walked to the cash machine, and a glittering pryamid of uncut diamonds had been swept into the call box where an eviscerated telephone dangled. Someone had passed in the night who loved the sound of breaking glass. She had been thinking about the possibilities of working in glass herself lately. She was an artist. Her cashpoint card bore the name Jessamy Jones; its number was a mnemonic of her children's birthdays. All grown up now, with children of their own. Jessamy had sketched their baby heads in tender pastels that stroked the curves of cheek and eye and ear and feathered hair; and a painting of them as children was sold as a postcard in the Tate. There was a wistful look about it, reminiscent of the nursery rhyme:

> Hark, hark, the dogs do bark,
> Beggars are coming to town.
> Some in rags and some in jags
> And one in a velvet gown.

Two people were waiting behind the man using the machine. Judging from the time he was taking, he was negotiating a mortgage, buying a pension plan, and making his will. The woman on his heels shifted her shopping bags and sighed; the boy lit a cigarette and looked murderous.

The autumn sunshine, gilding brick and berried trees, was benificent, like a matriarch bestowing gold and jewels on her heirs, all their sins forgiven; the plane trees were dappled benign giraffes. Jess stood a foot or so away to wait her turn, and looked down, on to cubes of viscous glass. She hadn't noticed them for years, but they must have been there all the time, those skylights set into pavements, the little squares of thick opaque glass letting out light from the cellars of shops, swimmy subaqueous light from the dank green cottages and gloomy caves of public conveniences. There was something she should have been thinking about, a decision to be made, but she stooped to study the tiles, seeing them with a child's eye, as if for the first time, pinkish, yellowish, greyish, dirtily opalescent, the colours of fish. Children are closer to the pavement, she was thinking, they know that the striped awning that encloses the greengrocer's emerald slope can suddenly snap in the wind and slap them in the face, that wooden cellar doors could fold back like heavy wings and plummet them into the underworld, that glass squares might hold more than bears.

Crouching there at a child's level, she heard a mother's voice: 'Will you shut up, or I'll give you something to cry for!' A howling infant was dragged past her. Something to cry for. That seemed doubly cruel, and unnecessary, as the child was already smeared and incoherent with an abundance of grief.

'You have no heart,' Jess had been told last night. 'You haven't got a heart.' Not true, not true. 'All you care about is your work.' There was a pretty iron grille above the skylight. 'You've got to decide. Come with me to America, or it's over.' Victorian, undoubtedly, the elaborate ironwork lattice. 'Crunch time' said the broken glass under people's feet. 'Make or break.'

48

Jessamy realised that she was squatting in the street and that she would be thought mad or drunk, if anyone noticed her at all; not that that bothered her, it was just that her knees were aching. She straightened up and looked into the shop window. From the back, in her huge sweater and jeans stiff with paint, she might have been a man, or girl, a woman or a boy; she was all of them, and none of them in particular when she worked. As she gazed, she realised the truth of the saying that charity begins at home; everything in this jumbled display had once been in somebody's home. An earlier proprietor's name was engraved in an ornamental strip across the top of the window: *Adèle. Coiffeuse and Wigmaker*: she must have been very sure of herself, to have her name incised in silvery Deco letters in the frosty glass. Where was Adèle now? The shop was closed and its interior dim; Jess saw her reflection doubled for an instant in the slightly distorted glass, as if another self had stepped sideways from her body and was looking at her. Beyond her selves, on a shelf, stood a light-fitting comprising three frilly-bottomed bells of crème brulée, as brittle as the caramelised topping that you crackle with your spoon. Was it camp, covetable kitsch, that brass-stemmed cluster, or BHS circa 1990? It was hard to tell. Jessamy knew that she had only to flick a switch, pull a string, and her life would be bathed in sweet toffee-coloured light. What to do? But look! The twin of the lustrous pearly globe, flecked blue and orange like a party balloon, that had been suspended on three chains from her childhood ceiling. Every so often Mother had stood on a chair to unhook it and empty it of its prey; daddy-long-legs, flies, moths, all silhouetted against the glass, and once, most horribly, a red admiral.

Decide. Make a decision. Decide whether or not to pick up the phone when you get home. Decide whether to sit beside someone in a Virgin aircraft, holding hands over

49

the Atlantic. She remembered holding up their entwined fingers, that seemed to float in the dusk above the bed, and saying 'our fingers make a candelabrum'. There, in the window, was a three-tiered cake stand, bordered in nasturtiums, with a tarnished fork, dating from the days when waitresses in white caps and aprons served cakes on decorous doileys, when the disseminated department store Bon Marché, down the road, had been the Harrods of South East London. She wondered if perhaps Adèle, looking down, ever paused in the Marcel waving of an angel's wing, and remembered. Over the noise of the traffic Jess could hear the boom and echoing crash of bottles being cast into the bottle bank, three council tumuli colour-coded Brown, White and Green.

Misbegotten garments, acrylic, fluorescent, trimmed with gilt and plastic, rubbed shoulders with the shrunken and drab in a brave, hopeless queue. A mildewed leather jacket brought a memory she would have preferred to forget, of a circle of Hell's Angels peeing on the brand-new leather jacket she had saved for months to buy, and on which she still owed money. That had been the initiation ceremony in which Jess was to be the official Old Lady of the leader of the pack. She had made her excuses and left. Well, fled in fact, pursued by burning brands and beer bottles. Her conversion to vegetarianism had come soon after, outside a butcher's shop. Tearing off the jacket, still smelly after repeated hosings and a trip to the dry cleaners, she had thrust it on a youth idling on a parked motorbike at the kerb.
'Here, take this jacket!' she had ordered, adding graciously, 'you can pee on it if you like.' He had vanished, vroom vroom, in a terrified trail of exhaust. She had gone home and applied to go to art school. The past, the past. What about the future? Was there a future in glass? Nobody was buying paintings; her last exhibition had

been well received but not a single painting had sold. Out of embarrassment she had stuck red dots on a few frames herself. Now she imagined herself in a booth at the end of a pier, twirling glass like spun sugar in the flame of a blow-torch, spinning the rigging of fragile ships, the legs of glass animals, fish with fissile fins, bambis with glaucoma. How did one go about getting such a job? Surely the position would be occupied by a gentle, bearded young man? Off the edge of the pier with him! – a faint hiss as a wave quenched and then closed over his bunsen burner.

'You've never loved anyone.' Not true. People from the past stepped forward to prove it. Then she saw that they were reflections in the shop window; perhaps she had always been looking in a mirror, watching others loving her? Damn. She had lost her place in the queue. The light would be quite gone by the time she got home. Two jacket potatoes would be splitting their sides in the oven waiting for her; Jess took as her example Piero di Cosimo, who had kept a bucket of boiled eggs beside him as he painted, so that he need not break off work to eat. As she was leaving the window, a flash of sapphire caught her eye, a shimmer of turquoise and flamingo pink. A powder compact with a lid of butterflies' wings under glass. There had been a shop window, long ago, filled with those vibrant wings made into pictures of silky tropical seas and black palm trees against savage sunsets; and set in silver jewellery, vivid on black velvet. If you looked closely you could see the veins in the wings.

Jessamy turned away angrily. Was this really what it was all about? Are we so imprinted in childhood, like orphaned ducklings who bond with wellington boots, or cartoon chicks squawking 'Mommy! That's my Mommy!' at exasperated wolves, that we spend the rest of our lives in pursuit of long-dead butterflies, chasing babyhood bunnies in an endless circle round and round the rim of a nursery bowl before sliding into the flames on a sledge

51

painted with a blistering rosebud? Look at the Harlequins. What colours, she wondered, would activate her children's nervous systems; some dress she herself had worn, a necklace of glass beads? What English *madeleine* rolled in coconut and topped with a *glacé* cherry would dissolve into memory in her lover's mouth? Then she speculated on whether we should love one another if we were made of glass, with all the workings visible, like transparent factories. We should have to; after all, we found beauty in eyes, ears and noses which were nothing but utilitarian. There was a boy going past, whose mouth was a more blatant organ than most, with his big fragile upper teeth puckering his lower lip like the skin of a deflating balloon. No heart? She could feel it heavy in her chest. She was all heart, had been from the start. Had she not been inconsolable when that pearly, flecked balloon had burst? It had had a pair of cardboard feet, and she had been left holding the disembodied feet in her hand. She had kept them for weeks. Did not spring evening skies of Indian ink drizzled over daffodil, or autumn sunsets like this one of apricot and sapphire, suffuse her with *tendresse*? She felt her eyes fill, the aqueous humour, the vitreous humour, glazed with tears. Decide if you want me in your life – a dear face fallen asleep over a book, spectacles slipping down a familiar nose, discs of glass magnifying closed eyelids veined like butterflies' wings.

At the bottle bank, a girl hesitated with a blue bottle in her hand, unsure where to deposit it, and as she held it up, blue as butterflies' wings from the Seychelles or the Philippines, Jess made her decision.

'Green!' she called. 'No, brown!'

Too late. The girl dropped it into the white bin. Blue on white. An arctic landscape. As Jess inserted her card, the cash dispenser's perspex eyelid closed in a slow malevolent wink as if to say 'I'll give you something to cry for.'

The glass squares in the pavement glowed faintly phosphorescent now. She looked down at one of them; old, adamantine, durable; it would take a pickaxe to break it.

The Curtain With The Knot In It

'You can see my window from here. It's the one with the curtain with the knot in it.'

Alice shivered, although the April late afternoon sun was turning the day room of Daffodil Ward into a greenhouse.

'Goose walked over your grave.' Pauline gave her abrupt laugh.

Alice looked out reluctantly across to the staff residential block, a three-storeyed cube of mottled brick, and located a dull curtain tied in a knot at a top-floor window.

Why, she wondered, had she shuddered like that? Was it the knot. Or the intimation that Pauline the Domestic had a life beyond Daffodil?

Pauline laughed again, at the antics of Jack, one of the patients, who had almost managed to slide under the tray that confined him to his chair.

'Come on Jack Be Nimble, Jack Be Quick,' she said as she pulled him back. 'You'll be having your soup in a minute.'

If a coypu were to laugh, Alice thought, or did she mean a capybara? Something with unattractive teeth and lank fur, unpopular with visitors at the zoo. The two women were of an age and dressed similarly, but with a world of difference between Alice's visitor's tracksuit and trainers and what was visible of Pauline's; pinkish-white and greyish-white peeking from under her nylon gingham overall. Pauline's hair hung limply from a rufflette of brown and yellow gingham, while Alice's was in a longish shiny bob.

Ada had been shouting from her chair for the curtains to be pulled since the rain had stopped and the sun had appeared two hours earlier, and now Sister was exasperated into swiping out spring with a swish of the orange curtains.

Alice's father had been wheeled into the ward so that something could be done to him, so she sat on a massive vinyl chair attempting to read a Large Print book whose pages had been glued together with Complan. Pauline went about her work, tearing sheets of pale blue paper from a large roll and slapping them down at each place on the long table, and on the trays of the chairs where the immobile were propped up on lolling and slipping pillows. Supper would not be served for an hour, but those who could Zimmer themselves there or who could be yanked and hoisted were seated at the table. Children's BBC blared on the television.

Anybody familiar with the tragedies, the dramas, the macabre comedies played out daily in places such as Daffodil, and the aching, aching boredom, the cross-purpose nature of every exchange will need no description of suppertime in this nursery of second childhood. Suffice it to say that it was a Wednesday and the big wooden calendar read *SUNDAY*, that the two budgies, presented by a well-wisher after the goldfish's suicide, twittered unregarded, that a voice called incessantly 'help me, help me, somebody please help me'; the never-opened piano and record player were there, and the floral displays in beribboned baskets, faded to the colour and texture of Rice Krispies, and in the side ward people who had died long ago were cocooned in cots and tended as if they might, some day, hatch into something marvellous, or exude skeins of wonderful silk.

When it became apparent that Dad had been put to bed, Alice went to say good night to him.

'Don't know why you bother coming every day,' said Pauline. 'He doesn't know you from a bar of soap, nemmind though, I've got a soft spot for your Dad myself.'

She was pouring powdered soup into the orange plastic beakers from an aluminium jug. George was spooning out his reconstituted bits of mushroom and laying them neatly on his blue paper. Mrs Rosenbaum didn't want any soup because she was dead.

'Aren't you staying for your tea tonight?' Pauline asked Alice.

'No, I'd better be going. Got a lot to do at home.'

She felt unequal to the nice milky one, two sugars, tonight. A misunderstanding early in their relationship made it impossible now for her to explain that she liked her tea black and unsweetened. 'I look after my *friends.*' Pauline would say darkly, with a pointed glance at Dolly's daughter who had unwittingly offended and was therefore not allowed tea. One of Alice's worst fears was that Dad would not die before Pauline's, as yet unspoken but looming, invitation to an off-duty cuppa in her flat.

Croxted Memorial, originally a cottage hospital, was built to a strange hexagonal design, with a small Outpatients and Casualty tacked on to one side, and even after a year of visiting, Alice could get lost, take a wrong turning and end up where she started or at the dead end of the permanently locked Occupational Therapy, or the kitchens with their aluminium vats and trolleys. The grey floor gleamed with little bubbles of disinfectant, a sign that read *Cleaning in Progress* half blocked her path, as it did every day although there were so few visitors or staff around that the place was like a morgue in the evenings, and there was Kevin the cleaner, leering over the handle of his heavy-duty polisher, pallid as a leek

56

with a tangle of pale dirty roots for hair. She knew she should have taken the other exit.

'Off out somewhere nice, are we?'

She gave a smile which tried to be enigmatic, distancing and hinting at a world beyond his overalls and disinfectant.

'When you coming out with me then?'

Alice pulled out her diary and flicked through the pages, aware of him squirming with incredulous lubricity.

'Let me see, I think I'm free on the twelfth.'

'You what . . .'

'Yes. The Twelfth of Never.' She snapped the diary shut triumphantly.

That was cruel, Alice, she admonished herself as she inhaled healing nicotine and evening air after the dead atmosphere which was Pauline's and Kevin's element, standing on the asphalt marled with white blossom while a blackbird sang in a cherry tree. Still, Kevin's idea of a venue for a good night out was probably that dark place behind the boiler room, where the wheelie bins lived.

Alice had lied to Pauline about having things to do, and deceived Kevin. The pages of her diary were almost all blank. Since she had been made redundant her world had shrunk until Daffodil and the long journeys by foot and tube and bus were her whole life. She no longer thought of herself as Alice at the Mad Hatter's tea party nearly as often as she had in the beginning. Her father, a Detective Inspector struck down and withered by illness over the years, was all the family she had and she loved him and grieved for his plight. She did not cry tonight; she had cried in so many hospital car-parks over the years.

Kevin watched her from the doorway, drawing deeply on a pinched roll-up. His glance went up to a window with a knotted curtain, billowing, deflated, in the wind that had sprung up, ruffling his hair.

*

Inside, in Daffodil, Pauline ruffled George's white hair as she collected his dishes.

'All right, Georgie Porgie?'

Writhing in agony from the pressure sore that was devouring him like an insatiable rodent, he drew back his lips in what Pauline took to be a smile.

'Pudding and Pie,' she added.

'You haven't eaten your sandwiches,' she accused Mrs Rosenbaum, whipping away the three triangles of bread and ham. When she had been brought in, Mrs Rosenbaum had tried to explain about eating kosher, but none of the staff or agency nurses had been able to take it on board, and she had shrunk into silence under her multi-coloured crochet blanket, while her feet swelled in the foam rubber boots fastened with velcro that Physio had provided, as slow starvation took its course.

The commodes that doubled as transport up the wooden hill to Bedfordshire were rolling into the day room.

'Come on Mary, Mary Quite Contrary,' said Sister Connelly as two of the Filipinos, they all looked the same to Pauline, and they never spoke to her anyway, started loading Mary on board. Quacking away in Foreign like a load of mandarin ducks. Thank God it was nearly time to knock off. She was really cheesed off today. Ada was singing, if you could call it that, "Ere we are again, 'Appy as can be. All good pals and JOLLY . . .' She always got stuck there.

'Change the record, Ada!' Pauline shouted as Ada started it up again.

'Pack it in, Joey. I've got a headache.' She told the budgies. 'Noisy buggers!'

'What are their names?' Alice had asked her once.

'I call them Joey. Can't tell them apart.' Pauline had replied.

'One's more emerald and the other's more turquoise.'

58

'You don't have to clear up after them!'

It was all right for some people with nothing better to do to go all soppy over a pair of budgies.

'I know why the caged bird sings,' Alice had said, but before she could go on Jack had tipped his chair over. Alice had had to sign a form as a witness, to show that there had been no negligence, after the doctor had been called, but that was the last they had heard of the matter.

Outside at last, Pauline had an impulse to take off her trainers and walk barefoot over the daisies in the grass, but Kevin was lurking around so she didn't. A blackbird was singing in the cherry tree, black against the white blossom. Pauline stood still for a moment, then, 'I've got a lot to do at home,' she said to herself and headed for the concrete stairs that led up to her flat. It was her thirty-seventh spring. Later that evening she went down to the payphone and dialled a number. She knew it by heart; it had stuck in her brain as soon as she had looked it up, and she had rung it many times. On the third ring Alice answered. Pauline hung up.

'Just having a chat with my mate,' she said as the dietician and his girlfriend came through the door in white tennis clothes with grass stains and a faint smell of sweat. They didn't look at her as they took the stairs two at a time, laughing at something. Pauline went slowly after them and finished off the last of the ham sandwiches from supper in Daffodil.

'She's gone, that little lady.' Pauline jerked a thumb towards the place where Mrs Rosenbaum had sat. It was the following afternoon. Alice made her heart blank, and looked down at her book.

'Having a nice read?'

Pauline tipped the book forward. 'Janette Turner Hospital. She must be the same as me.'

'She's Australian, I think.' Alice didn't want to be too much of a know-all.

'No, I mean, she must've been found in a hospital, like me. I was left in the toilets at Barts, that's why they give me the name. Pauline after the nurse who found me, and Bartholomew after Barts. 'Ee-ah, nice milky one, two sugars.'

'Thanks, Pauline, you're a pal.'

As she drank her tea, Alice realised that she had been given the central fact about Pauline. That beginning had determined her progression to this institutional job, that overall, the trolley, the table for one in Spud-U-Like, the holidays spent in shopping precincts.

'I had my picture in all the papers,' said Pauline, and Alice saw a crimson, new-born baby waving feeble arms from swaddling clothes of newsprint, on a stone floor under a porcelain pedestal.

'Your mother – did they – did she?'

Pauline's eyes filled as she shook her head, strands of hair whipping her clamped mouth. 'I've never told anybody that before. Nobody here, I mean. Not that they'd be interested anyway, toffee-nosed lot.'

Alice had noticed that the staff hardly gave Pauline a glance or a word. Poor, despised capybara, whose cage everybody walked past.

That revelation led to Alice's following Pauline up the concrete stairs after visiting time, with a sense of danger knowing she had taken an irrevocable step. She hadn't know how to refuse the long-threatened invitation after Pauline's tears. To her horror Pauline at once took an unopened bottle of Tia Maria from a cupboard in the tiny kitchen, which was a scaled-down replica of the kitchenette at Daffodil.

'Ah, the curtain with the knot in it! At last!' Alice cried, a bit too gaily, as they carried their glasses through.

'Tell me, Pauline, why does it have a knot in it?'

'I'm a fresh-air fiend. All the cooking smells from foreign cooking get trapped in here so I leave my window open and I have to tie the curtain back or it knocks my ornaments off in the wind.'

'I'd imagined a much more sinister – I mean exotic – explanation, but I see your balloon-seller's head has been glued back on at some stage.'

Pauline topped them up.

'Mind if I smoke?' Alice asked.

'That's all right, I'll get the ash tray.'

It had been washed but Alice detected a smear of grey under its rim which indicated that Pauline had at least one other visitor, who smoked.

'It's a lovely flat, Pauline. A little palace. You've made it really homely.'

'It is home.'

'Well yes, of course.'

'You haven't seen the bedroom yet, have you?'

Alice gasped. Fifty pairs of eyes stared at her from the bed; the big eyes of pink and yellow and white and turquoise fluffy toys, and squinting eyes of trolls with long fluorescent hair.

'Meet the Cuddlies,' said Pauline. 'Sometimes I think they're more trouble than all my patients put together.'

Alice felt sudden fear, of all the goggle-eyes, the garish nylon fibres, strong enough to strangle. Pauline had lured her here to kill her. Get her drunk on Tia Maria and do away with her. In cahoots with Kevin.

'What a wonderful collection. Well, I suppose I'll have to think about going, Pauline. Long journey and all that.' Oh God. That was the mistake people always made in films; saying they were going instead of just making a run for it when the murderer was off-guard.

'Oh, I was going to do us a pizza. Won't take a minute in the microwave.' Pauline was bitterly disappointed. That was what friends did, ate pizza on the sofa in front

61

of the telly. Then her face broke into a smile when Alice said, 'OK, great. Thanks, that would be lovely. Mind if I use your loo?'

'Help yourself.'

As Alice left the room she paused, 'Pauline, mind if I ask you something? Kevin, are you and he . . .I mean does he come here sometimes?'

'Not often.' Pauline was upset at the intrusion of Kevin into the evening. 'I let him come up once in a while. Only when I'm really browned-off.'

Cheesed-off. Browned-off. Alice had an image of Pauline's brown and yellow overall bubbling in a microwaved Welsh Rarebit.

Pauline put Kevin out of her mind and went into the kitchen as Alice closed the bathroom door behind her. She selected two pizzas from the tiny freezer and got a sharp knife from the drawer to score along the marked quarters. The doorbell rang.

Alice, in the bathroom with her ear to the wall, heard the freezer door slam, and the metallic scrape of cutlery. The doorbell. In total panic she wrenched open the bathroom door. Kevin stood inside the front door, blocking the way. And Pauline had a long knife in her hand.

Alice made a rush for the door, shoving Kevin out of the way but Pauline was right behind her, grabbing the back of her sweatshirt, saying, 'Alice, wait! What about the pizzas?' Alice was pulled round, and for black moments all three were struggling together in the narrow hallway in a tangle of bodies and knife. Then the knife got shoved in. Five inches of stainless steel straight to the heart.

They looked at her lying there. There was no question that she was dead.

'Bloody hell,' said Kevin. 'I only come up for a cup of sugar.'

It occurred to neither of them to call the police.

'I'll have to get her bagged-up,' said Kevin then.

The Domestic was red-eyed and shaky in the morning as she handed out the breakfasts. She looked as if she'd been awake all night. She had; the accusing whispers of the Cuddlies had not let up. She could hear them still through her open window as she crossed the grass, the window with the curtain with the knot in it. Her hair was lank and uncombed under her scrunched rufflette of gingham, but nobody gave her a glance anyway.

'Come on Dolly Daydream, let's be having you,' she said with her abrupt mirthless laugh. 'Tea up. Nice milky one, two sugars.'

Once, not so long ago, Alice's father, the former Detective Inspector, who was trained to observe, would have looked up with a pleased, though puzzled, smile sensing something amiss as she handed him his tea. She had always had a soft spot for him too, but now he didn't know her from a bar of soap.

Cloud-Cuckoo-Land

The Rowleys glowed in the dark. On wet winter mornings
Muriel was fluorescent, streaming in the rain like a
lifeboatperson with a lollipop guiding children over the
big crossroads where the lights, when they were working,
controlled twelve streams of traffic. As often as not there
was an adhesive lifeboat somewhere about her person for
her coat and cap were studded with stickers, bright and
new, peeling and indecipherable, of any good cause you
could mention, and grey smudges were the ghosts of
charities which had achieved their aims, given up or been
disbanded in disgrace. Her husband Roy had reflective
strips on his bicycle pedals, and his orange cape and
phosphorescent armbands, his rattling collection tins of
all denominations were a familiar sight outside super-
markets, at car boot sales and in the station forecourt.
There were neighbours who doused the lights and television and dropped to the floor if they had warning of his
approach, but most people preferred to give, if only a few
pesetas or drachmas, because everyone knew the Rowleys
would do anything for anybody. A landslide victory in the
local radio station poll had earned them its Hearts of Gold
Award, and they had been presented with a box of Terry's
All Gold Chocolates, a catering-size jar of Gold Blend
coffee and a bouquet of yellow lilies with pollen like curry
powder. In a different household the permanence of the
stamens' dye, staining the wall behind the vase, a heap of

books, a clutch of raffle tickets and a pile of laundry might have been a minor disaster.

Visitors to number 35 Hollydale Road, having cleared the assault course of the little hall, Roy and Muriel's stiff PVC and nylon coats, the bicycles which still wore the red noses of that charitable bonanza, Red Nose Day of a few years back, boxes of books, dented tins of catfood and jumble and birdseed, stacks of newspaper tied with string, turned left into the front room, where Roy was, this early afternoon, occupied in sorting through a pile of *National Geographics*. Since his retirement from the buses he had been so busy that now he joked about going back to work for a holiday, although he did put in two mornings a week at the Sue Ryder shop. One of his regular passengers had written a letter once to the *Evening Standard* praising his cheerfulness and he had enjoyed a brief fame as 'the whistling conductor'; people had queued up to ride on his bus. 'The Lily of Laguna' had been his favourite, and 'I Believe', and 'What a Wonderful World', until a polyp on his throat had put paid to that. Roy was an autodidact who had left school at fourteen and was now a gaunt man whose hair stuck up in black and grey tufts; his teeth protruded and his bare ankles, between the cuffs of his navy blue jogging pants and his brogues, were bony. There were traces in him still of the little boy in the balaclava waiting for the library to open, and the skinny eager student at the WEA. He was squinting at the close print of the magazines through a pair of glasses picked from a pile awaiting dispatch to the Third World and now and then a brown breast zonked him in the eye. There was not a surface in the room uncovered by papers, propaganda and paraphernalia. He was distracted by a movement past the window and glanced up to see old Mr and Mrs Wood from 43 creeping along to the shops with their bags inflated by the late October nor'easter. He

65

noted how frail they had become with the end of summer. The clocks went back that weekend.

'"The Woods decay, the Woods decay and" – Muriel!' He shouted her name. 'Muriel! The Woods have had a fall!'

Muriel rushed through from the kitchen, was tripped up by a bale of newspapers and kicked on the ankle by a bicycle, and saw Roy kneeling beside the Woods who were stretched out on the pavement, as two white plastic bags drifting along were inflated by a gust of wind and tossed like balloons into the branches of an ornamental maple. Punching the familiar digits on her mobile phone, Muriel summoned an ambulance, and hurried, her blue acrylic thighs striking sparks off each other, to wrench open Walter Wood's beige jacket with a sound of ripping velcro, and pinch his purple nose and clamp her mouth to his blue lips. Roy was attending to Evelyn Wood.

'Don't try to struggle,' he soothed her, 'the ambulance is on its way.'

When it arrived, the Woods were covered with a grubby double duvet and a scattering of yellow leaves.

'Got the Babes in the Wood for you, Keith,' Muriel called out to the ambulance crew, who were old friends and soon had the Woods strapped comfortably on board.

'He slipped on – something slippery,' Roy explained, 'and took her down with him. They came a fearful cropper. I saw it happen.' As Keith closed the doors a voice came from within:

'Monstrous . . . two world wars . . . Passchendaele, Givenchy, Vimy Ridge . . .' and was cut off by the siren.

The onlookers went indoors, three subdued young mothers with pushchairs ambled on and curtains fell back into place as the blue light turned the corner. Muriel gave the duvet a shake and headed home to replace it in the bedroom as Roy surreptitiously scuffed a few more leaves over the condom he kicked into the gutter, the slimy cause of Walter's downfall. He felt sick. It was not the sort of thing you expected in Hollydale Road, a pallid invader from a diseased and alien culture.

'Don't suppose we'll be seeing them back in Hollydale; Roy predicted in the kitchen.

'No. Here – I've made us some nice hot Bovril – I expect they'll be sent to Selsdon Court eventually. Hopefully. Still, perhaps its a blessing it happened when it did, before the bad weather. I do worry about the old folk in the winter, when the pavements are icy.'

Roy dunked a flapjack into his Bovril and sucked it. The Rowleys were such good sports that if anyone found a half-baked raffle ticket or a paper rose or a lifeboat in one of Muriel's cakes they took it in good part, although among the cognoscenti it was a case of 'once bitten . . .'

'No word, I suppose, Mummy?'

Roy nodded towards the breadbin. 'I would have said. Still, she may have tried to ring – you know how busy the phone is.'

A subdued hooting came from the bathroom.

'Drat that barn owl!' exclaimed Muriel. 'Doesn't seem to know it's supposed to be nocturnal! Where does it think I'm going to get fresh vermin from at this time of day? That's something they don't tell you in those wildlife documentaries. Its beak's well mended now, thanks to that superglue, but it obviously has no intention of taking itself off, thank you very much! Knows which side *its* bread's buttered – well, I suppose I'd better fetch him down,' she concluded with maternal resignation.

As Muriel went upstairs the portable phone rang from the draining board.

'Helpline Helpline. My name's Roy. Is there a problem you'd like to talk about? Something you want to share?'

A gruff throat was cleared.

'Take your time,' Roy encouraged. 'I'm here to listen when you're ready to talk . . .'

Helpline Helpline had been established to counsel

people addicted to ringing, or setting up, Helplines. Roy and Muriel had been roped in to man the local branch.

'When did you first begin to think you might have a problem?' As Muriel came in with Barney on her shoulder, and Roy motioned her to be quiet, a hoarse monotone was saying truculently,

'The Bisexual Helpline was busy, so I dialled this number.'

'I'm glad you did – um – could you tell me your name, any name will do, this is all in the strictest confidence of course – it just makes it easier for us to communicate. I said I'm Roy, didn't I?'

Barney was swooping towards him, sinking talons into his shoulder. Roy winced.

'Leslie.'

'So, Leslie – is that with an 'ie' or a 'y' by the way? Not important – you're having a bit of trouble with your bicycle are you? What's the problem, gears lights, mudguards? Well, we can get that sorted, and then, if you feel up to it, we can address the subtext of your cry for help, i.e., why are you hooked on helplines, and how we at Helpline Helpline can – excuse me a moment, Lesley don't go away – I've got a barn owl on my shoulder –'

'And I've got a monkey on my back,' said the caller and hung up.

'Damn! I was just making the Breakthrough. We'll really have to make a determined effort to return Barney to his own environment. At the weekend, maybe. After the Mini Fun Run.'

He picked up the sandwich Muriel put down on the table and was opening his mouth when Muriel said, 'Don't eat that, it's Barney's. Worm and Dairylea.' A silence fell and each knew the other was thinking of their own chick who had flown the nest. Who would have imagined, least of all themselves, that the Rowleys would have a daughter who would be decanted on to the doorstep by disgruntled cab

68

drivers at all hours, and who had now taken up with a Jehovah's Witness? They had fallen out with Petula over the issue of blood transfusion; as operations and transfusions were, so to speak, Roy's and Muriel's lifeblood, it was a vexed question. Giving blood was part of their credo. They had medals for it. There were gallons of Roy's and Muriel's blood walking around in other folk.

Roy put his arms round Muriel, feeling pleasant stirrings of desire as man, wife and owl formed an affectionate tableau, until Muriel felt sharp claws rake her trouser-leg.

'Look who's feeling left-out, then. Come on, Stumpy. Come on, darling.'

She sat down with the cat on her knee. Roy adjusted the drawstring of his jogging pants.

'We're not allowed to call him Stumpy any more, according to the Politically Correct lobby. No, we must henceforth refer to our truncated companion as 'horizontally challenged . . .'

'What *is* your daddy on about now?' Muriel asked the cat.

'Like calling him Nigger.'

'Why on earth would we? He's a tabby tomtom, aren't you pet? Nigger was *black*, you daft thing. Well, this won't get the baby a new frock . . . I promised to pick up Mrs B's prescription and pension before lollipop time.

As Muriel popped on her mac the phone went and she heard Roy answer 'Helpline Helpline'.

Petula Rowley had once told her father that whenever she heard him explain to a new acquaintance or a reporter from the local media how he had been 'bitten by the Charity Bug', she saw a large striped glossy beetle rattling a collecting tin at her. She had added that she felt like stamping on that antlered stag and colorado hybrid; but she herself had been the unwitting cause of her parents' metamorphosis from an unremarkable, well-disposed but uncommitted youngish couple into the baggy-trousered philanthropists of the present day. When Petula was five the Educational Psychologist, called in by her worried headmistress, had diagnosed a boredom threshold at danger level, and it was as therapy that Muriel and Roy had enrolled their little daughter, all the more precious now for her handicap, in a dancing class which put on shows in old people's homes and hospitals. Not very long after the family had been barred from Anello & Davide where they bought Petula's ballet shoes, those expensive pale pink pumps like two halves of a seashell, Petula had refused to attend the class. Muriel took her to the Tate to see Degas' *Little Dancer* in her immortal zinc tulle to no avail and they were requested to leave the gallery. Muriel had Petula's ballet shoes cast in bronze anyway. They posed on top of the television for years until somehow, without anybody really noticing, they became an ashtray, and later a repository for paperclips and elastic bands. Petula had defected, but her parents were well and truly hooked on Charity. Was it the smell of hospitals or of tea steaming from battered urns that got them; the smiles on old people's faces or the laughter of sad children, or the cut-and-thrust of the committee meeting where Roy could be relied on to come up with 'Any Other Business' or one more Point of Order, just when folk were putting on their coats with thoughts of the adjacent hostelry? He was proud to share his initials with Ralph Reader of Gang Show fame; the Rowleys had ridden along on the crest of a wave, and Petula was dragged behind in the undertow, her boredom threshold quite forgotten.

As Roy returned to the task of sorting the magazines, contributions to the next car boot at Stella Maris, the school whose pupils Muriel escorted across the road, he was conscious of the discomfort in his chest; the pain of estrangement from his daughter that Milk of Magnesia couldn't shift. The Third World spectacles slid down his

70

nose and fell to the floor, and as he picked them up a tiny screw rolled out and the tortoise shell leg came away in his hand. Roy groped another pair with heavy black frames from the pile and put them on. The room lurched at him, furniture, window glass and frame and the trees outside zooming into his face as he turned his head. He sat down, seasick, in a huge armchair.

As the nausea passed Roy became aware of a thick grey cobweb slowly spiralling from the lightshade in the centre of the ceiling, saw that the shade itself, which he remembered as maroon, was furred by dust and trimmed with dead woolly bear caterpillars, and that loops and swags of cobweb garlanded the picture rails, tags of sellotape marked Christmases past and a balloon had perished and melted long ago, and soot and dust had drifted undisturbed into every cornice and embossment of the anaglypta wallpaper. Curled, yellowing leaflets and pamphlets and press-cuttings ringed with coffee stains were all about him, a pile of grubby laundry on the stained sofa, something nasty on the sleeve of the Live Aid record, unplayed because they had nothing on which to play it; his knees were blue mountains with a growth of Stumpy's fur, and downy featherlets caught in a dried-up stream of Bovril. Then his ankles! Roy could not believe the knobs and nodules below the fringe of black-grey foliage, the wormcasts and bits of dead elastic, the anatomical red and blue threads and purple starbursts. 'These aren't my feet,' he said. 'Some old man has made off with Roy Rowley's feet while he wasn't looking and dumped these on me.'

> Other people's babies – that's my life.
> Mother to do-ozens but nobody's wife!

Roy heard a voice singing at the front door and then a key in the lock, and then a yoo-hoo and then some old girl was in the room shrugging off a sulphurous yellow coat banded with silver, and waving a virulent green lollipop, like a traffic light on a stick, under his nose.

'Yum yum, piggy's bum, you can't have none,' she taunted in imitation of a child's voice, popping the green glassy ball into her mouth, with the stick protruding. She crunched glass and glooped the ball out with a pop.

'One of my little boyfwends gave it to me,' she lisped, and started to sing 'We are the lollipop kids' like an overgrown Munchkin, then stopped. Roy was staring at the great, bobbly pink and grey diamonds on her jumper, the greasy grey elf-locks on her shoulders. It was he who had made her promise never to cut her hair short – how long ago had that been?

'Why are you staring at me like that? You look as if you've seen a ghost – or have I got something on my face?'

'No – not really. I've seen it advertised in the paper, you can get some shampoo-stuff – I mean a gadget for shaving sweaters. It removes all the pills and bobbles – it brings them up like new . . .'

'What pills and bobbles? What are you talking about now? What does?' He had made her feel silly about the lollipop.

'This gizmo I was telling you about.'

All her pleasure in the sweet was gone.

'I reckon it's you who could do with a shave,' she said and waddled – no, this was his beloved Muriel – walked out of the room.

'Mummy,' he called after her.

'I'm going to see about Barney's tea.'

Roy walked over to the mirror which hung on a chain on the wall above the cluttered mantelpiece and breathed on it and rubbed a clear patch on its clouded glass. Grey quills were breaking the surface of his skin and there was an untidy tuft half-way down his neck; he was scrawny and granular, his nose was pitted like a pumice stone;

and hadn't he seen an ad for another gadget too, for trimming the ears and nose?

'I look a disgrace,' he observed wonderingly. 'A tramp. A scarecrow in a pigsty – that I thought was a palace.' It was like some fairy-tale featuring a swineherd or a simpleton who, ungrateful for his sudden riches, found himself back in his squalid hut; but was the world he saw through the black glasses a distortion, or reality to which he had been blind?

'Getting vain in our old age, are we?' Muriel, good humour evidently restored, had returned. 'When you've finished titivating yourself, I've brought you a cup of tea.'

A hand like a cracked gardening glove seamed with earth was thrusting a pink mug at him; he saw the stained chip on its lip and the tea oozing through the crack that ran down its side.

'Ta muchly, love,' he said weakly, lowering himself carefully on to the chair.

'You look different,' commented Muriel.

'So do you,' he thought.

'I can't put my finger on it.'

She studied him, her great face in cruel-close up going from side to side. Roy was beginning to get a headache. Muriel had slipped her feet into a pair of pom-pommed mules and the rosehip scarlet dabs of varnish which time had pushed to the tips of her big toenails marked the end of summer.

'When I've had this, I'd better get the rest of those Save Our Hospital leaflets through some more doors,' he said. 'Shouldn't take too long. What are we having for supper?'

Muriel's mouth concertinaed in hurt wrinkles. Friday night was Dial-A-Pizza and early-to-bed night; a bottle of Black Tower was chilling in the fridge above the owl food.

'Is there any aspirin, love? I think I'm getting one of my heads.'

Muriel dipped into her pockets and tore off a strip of Aspro. He swallowed two tablets the size of extra-strong peppermints. By the time Roy was walking back up Hollydale, his leaflets distributed by lamplight without the aid of spectacles, his head was clear.

'I've got a bone to pick with you!'

It was Mr Wood shouting from the doorway of 43. Roy hurried across, surprised and pleased to see the old boy home and on his feet but guilty that he hadn't telephoned the hospital to enquire. Walter Wood's face was purple in the porchlight and he was gesticulating at a padded neck brace that held his head erect.

'I hold you responsible for this!' he was shouting.

'Me?'

The french letter slithered into Roy's mind.

'Me?' Roy repeated. Not guilty, surely?

'Yes you! If you and your do-gooding wife hadn't been so keen to bundle us off to the knacker's yard – we were just a bit shaken, getting our breaths back – and you might advise your better half to lay off the vindaloo if she's going to make a habit of giving the so-called kiss of life! They kept us lying on trolleys in the corridor for hours, like a pair of salt cod – couldn't even go to the toilet. I got such a crick in my neck they had to issue me with this!' he thumped his surgical collar. 'The wife's got one too. She's worse off than I am because they had to commandeer a trolley from the kitchen for her. She's up in the bathroom now, trying to wash the smell of soup and custard out of her hair. I doubt she'll ever look a cooked dinner in the face again.'

He pointed to the frosted bathroom window and Roy became aware of the sound of water gurgling down the drainpipe.

'You and your everlasting charity! You want to come down to earth and do something about that front garden of yours, it's a disgrace to the street! You're living in Cloud-Cuckoo-Land, my friend!'

A Save Our Hospital leaflet was flung as Roy retreated, and was sucked back into the purple vortex of Walter Wood's rage, plastering itself across his face.

Indoors, having slunk through the fluffy Michaelmas daisy seed-heads of his shamed garden, Roy resolved to try a different pair of spectacles, but the multi-eyed heap of insects was gone.

'The Brownies came for them while you were out,' Muriel told him.

A fey image of little folk batting at the window with tiny hands and fleeing with their haul through the falling leaves startled him. I'd better watch my denture in case the Tooth Fairy gets any ideas, he thought, but said that he was going to have a quick bath before the pizzas came. If the Rowleys had been less charitable, a visit to the optician would have been taken for granted; as finances stood, Roy decided to buy a pair off the peg at the chemist as soon as he had time. He put on the black-framed glasses to go upstairs and felt at once the strain as his eyes were pulled towards the huge lenses, and the giant staircase reared in front of him.

He surveyed the bathroom – a locker room after the worst rugby team in the league had departed to relegation, he thought, as he picked at the guano of owl droppings and toothpaste on the mirror. Once immersed with antiseptic Radox emeralds dissolving around him, he felt better, lifted the dripping sponge, squeezed it over his head and began to sing, gruffly:

> I believe for every drop of rain that falls,
> A flower grows.
> I believe that somewhere in the darkest night
> A candle glows . . .
> Every time I see a newborn baby die . . .

75

Good God! He started again.

> Every time I hear a newborn baby cry,
> Or touch a leaf, or see the sky —
> Then I know why
> I believe.

Roy Rowley with a packet of seeds and a bundle of gardening tools versus desert sands unfertilised by innumerable millions of bones.

'I believe that every time I take a bath,
A river dries.
I believe . . . NO!
I believe that Someone in that Great Somewhere hears — how absurd!'

Terrified, he stuffed the sponge into his mouth.

'Never mind, lovey, there's always next Friday,' Muriel consoled him in bed. 'It happens, or doesn't if you get my meaning, to the best of men at times.'

'How would she know?' Roy wondered bitterly. Barney's great glassy yellow eyes winked lewdly from the top of the wardrobe. Stumpy was sniffing a circle of pepperoni stuck to the lid of the box beside the bed.

'He likes it but it doesn't like him!' Muriel informed Roy.

'I know.'

Roy woke late with a headache and the fleeing remnants of a dream in which he and Muriel were being turned down as foster parents. The smell of frying bacon curled round his nose and he could hear Muriel's and Barney's muted voices.

'Tu-whit, tu-whoo — a merry note, while greasy Joan doth keel the pot.' He thought.

When he barged into the kitchen wearing the glasses

the phone rang. Sidestepping Muriel's morning kiss, Roy picked it up.

'Yes?'

'Oh. Um, I must've got the wrong number. I thought this was the Helpline . . .'

'It is. Got a problem ringing helplines have you, pal? Well, try a bit of aversion therapy – piss off! There that should put you off wasting your own time and everybody else's!'

Muriel was open-mouthed with a rasher sliding from the fork suspended in her hand. Roy removed the spectacles; he had seen that the kitchen, the heart of the home, was splattered with the grease of thousands of marital breakfasts, and shoals of salmonella swam upstream to mate and lay their eggs. Anxiety from his oneiric ordeal crackled in static electricity from the viscose stripes of his dressing-gown, caused horripilation of the pyjama-ed limbs, itching of the feet in furry socks and irritation of the scalp. He and Muriel had been unpleasantly accused, judged, condemned in his dream, he remembered with shock that he had been sentenced to some kind of heavy-labouring Community Service for which he had been late, miles away, attempting to read the time on somebody's large upside-down watch. He had been trying to conceal his disgrace from Petula, desperate not to lose her respect, so that she might still turn to him as a daughter to a father. Owl's beak chomped unspeakable morsel, Muriel departed in yellow to take a partially-sighted friend shopping, Saturday got under way. He had to put the glasses on to examine the pile of post. The fowls of the air, the fish and mammals of the sea, the North Sea itself besought Roy Rowley of Hollydale Road to save them. An ancient Eastern European face under a head-scarf howled in grief and told Roy that winter was coming and there was no end to the killing and no food and no shelter from the snow. Roy thrust all their pleadings into

77

the breadbin. Nothing of course from Petula. Stumpy was importuning for a second breakfast. As Roy spooned a lump of catfood into his bowl, some slithered over his hand. It felt curiously warm to the touch although the tin was almost at its sell-by date. The red buttocks of a tomato squatting on a saucer caught his eye. Roy sliced and ate it quickly, for if his new vision were to encompass lascivious thoughts towards fruit and veg he was lost. He could see Petula in a pink dress standing by the piano in a church hall piping 'Jesus bids us shine with a pure clear light, like a little candle burning in the night. In this world of darkness, we must shine. You in your small corner, and I in mine.' There was a ten-bob note in her heart-shaped pocket, but it had been worth it to hear the collective 'Aaah' when she skipped on to the stage.

There was no possibility of a visit to the chemist that day. The Mini Fun Run took over entirely. 'Why do they do it?' Roy questioned in the autumnal park, stopwatch in hand, as agonised red and purple thighs juddered past him, and breasts were thrown about in coloured vests. 'The world need never have known. Whatever happened to feminine mystique?'

To his left an aerobics class in very silly costumes was performing a display. How sad to think of them entering sports shops to purchase those garments and then, in the privacy of their own homes, dressing up in those clinging silver suits under magenta bathing costumes, and matching headbands and wristlets, to step on and off jogging machines and hone their muscles on mail-order Abdomenisers and Thighmasters. A police dog was trying to rip the padded arm off an officer disguised as a criminal in a rival attraction; sales of curried goat and rice, burgers, kebabs and Muriel's Rice Krispie cakes were steady; the event was a success even though the mini hot-air balloon Roy had booked let him down. Muriel, in the grey livery of the St John Ambulance Brigade was tending to a bungee jumper who had come to grief. Soon be Guy Fawkes, and she'd be on the Front Line again. Roy was booked for the Scouts Sausage Sizzle. Suddenly he had no taste for it. He'd rather just stay indoors, worrying about other people's pets.

At the last moment, that evening, Muriel felt that she could not face the rehabilitation of Barney, and Roy set out alone on his bicycle with the owl in a duffel bag and an ersatz Tupperware box of bits and pieces that were to be scattered around the new habitat.

'I'll just stay here and have a good 'owl,' Muriel had told him, 'I only hope he gets acclimatised before bonfire night.' and bravely waved a scrunched Kleenex as he pedalled away. She had sent her annual letter to the local paper reminding people to check their bonfires for slumbering hedgehogs.

'He was out of that duffel bag like a cork from a bottle, Mummy, was our boy. I caught hold of him for a moment and he looked me right in the eye as if to say, 'Thank you, Uncle Roy and Aunty Muriel for having me, but I'm an endangered species and it's up to me now to do my bit in the conservation and breeding stakes.' I tossed him gently into the air and he took to it like – a duck to water! I don't mind admitting, Mummy, I was quite moved – that poem, you know. 'Everyone suddenly burst out singing', came into my mind when I saw him rise above the treetops, silhouetted against the crescent moon.'

'What's that tapping sound? That tap tap tap on the window?' Muriel said sharply.

It was a strand of jasmine, come loose from its pin.

Then he saw that she had all Petula's old photos out, the baby pictures and school portraits and holiday snaps.

That night Roy couldn't sleep. 'Do-Gooders' Walter Wood had called them, tarnishing the Hearts of Gold Award. I do try to do good, he thought, is that so wrong? Then he was in the day room of the Sunshine Ward at the threatened hospital, tickling the yellowed ivories of the old joanna: 'The way you wear your hat, the way you drink your tea . . . the memory of all that . . . no, no, they can't take that away from me . . .' and he looked around his captive audience, hatless and uncomprehending and at the spouted feeding cup from which an old boy sucked his tea and knew that, yes, they could take everything away.

If they took away his charity work, if he were to stop running from errand of mercy to good deed and stand still, what would Roy Rowley be? An empty tracksuit filled with air? He snuggled up to Muriel's back and his bony fingers rested on gently rising and falling pneumatic flesh, aware of her dedicated, donated organs working a quiet night-shift. But what if that pump which drove them should suddenly stop and he feel no movement under his terrified hand?

Sunday, and an urban cockerel, gardens away, dissolved brick and asphalt in the morning mist as Roy lay in bed, reluctant to leave its safety, and took him back to the muddy green rural outskirts of Orpington of his boyhood. Sometimes in late autumn the birds sing as if they were on the verge of spring rather than winter, and Roy listened dully to their songs thinking about the city built in the air by the birds, where Walter Wood had accused him of living. If only. He could see, on the chair, an empty blue-grey nylon harness and a deflated pair of Y-fronts. O black lace and shiny ribboned rayon and white cotton, when that Lloyd Loom linen basket with the glazed lid was new! The sheets in which he lay, once yellow, had come, like the fibreglass curtains, from Brentford Nylons in the days when he and Muriel had thought it posh, when they had paused for a moment each time they entered the bedroom to admire that flounced valance and

80

the kidney-shaped dressing table's matching skirt. He itched, and longed for the touch and scent of sun and wind-dried cotton. Soon he must face the day through those dystopic lenses. He was not going to church this morning, although Muriel was, having a standing arrangement to push one of the old girls from Selsdon Court, the sheltered accommodation to which she had prematurely consigned the Woods. Roy would be on parade in a couple of weeks, on Remembrance Sunday, in his Rover Scouts uniform, and Walter Wood would be there in his medals. Roy had been demobbed undecorated from his National Service. His memories were of boils on the neck and skin chafed to a raw rash by khaki, and blisters. Walter Wood's protest as he was carried away to the ambulance came back to Roy as he shaved – the roll call of Great War battles. Roy dreaded the service at the war memorial now; feared that the fallen might look down on those they had died to defend and reckon their sacrifice futile: Fall in, you rusty tins of Andrews with your lids jammed half-open in an eternal grin; Present Arms, you broken-handled verdigrised half-spoons and clogged-up combs; To the left, wheel!, Optrex eyebaths and tubigrips and old blue unopened rolls of bandage. Atten-shun Germolene and Brolene and haemorrhoid cream and Dentu-creme, the packet of razor blades rotted to the shelf, the nest of Kirbigrips, the melted square of Ex-lax, the cloudy dregs of Aqua-Velva.

He went to breakfast to find that some small girls had brought Muriel an injured woodpigeon in a box. She handed Roy a plate of bacon, eggs and beans. She was dressed for church in a turquoise leisure suit. A deckle-edged snapshot of his parents was flashed past his eyes: Mother in a grey costume with white gloves, Father in pinstripes, both wearing hats. He acknowledged his own Sunday attire, a clownish suit that would have baffled them and cost them about a month's wages.

81

'I'll pop Woody in the old rabbit hutch when I go out,' she said.

'We should call him Herman or Guthrie,' said Roy, fighting his vision of humankind as worth no more than the contents of its collective bathroom cabinet, the grey underwear hiding under its bright uniforms. Muriel smiled.

'Or Allen,' he added.

'Ooh no! You won't forget the boot sale, will you lovey?' Roy could feel the dull pain of Petula's loss as he ate, and stifled a burp in his kitchen-roll serviette.

'Pardon me for being rude, it was not me, it was my food,' he said mechanically.

The bare twiggy branches of the trees stuck up in witches' brooms as Roy walked down the road, the fallen leaves of a magnolia grandiflora lay like bits of brown leather; old shoes. A van was parking in the forecourt of the council estate and two masked men in yellow protective clothing got out carrying fumigating equipment. There was a mattress lying on top of a heap of rags and Roy saw, and recoiled from, had to look again in hopeful disbelief then horror, the sodden outline of what had once been a human being rotted to the stained ticking. Those men in yellow; they and their kind were the ones who really knew how the world worked, and kept it going. He stood, what else could he do, a well-intentioned bloke in an anorak; a drone. And of course they, those yellow ones, were the most respected and rewarded members of the community for what they did, weren't they? Like hell they were.

At the car boot he delivered his magazines and sundry other goods and strolled round the playground with a notion of picking up a better pair of glasses, and stopped in front of a blanket on the ground. It was a thin tartan car rug and the goods displayed were a baby's dummy, two feeding bottles with perished teats, a splayed-out wire and nylon bottle brush, some Anne French cleansing milk, two pairs of pop-sox in unopened packs, a pair of jeans and a tube of coloured bath pearls. Roy paid for the bath pearls with a five pound note, guessing the young woman would be unable to change it. Three children with purple smudges under their eyes and the necks of baby birds watched silently.

'Don't worry about it. Some other time,' he said and hurried away blushing to the roots of his tufty hair, with the bath pearls in his hand. Petula used to like the red ones; when she was little she would burst one and squash it against her arm or leg in the bath, and then scream, 'Help! Help! I've cut myself really badly!' and bring Mummy and Daddy rushing in panic. They fell for it every time.

'Royston!' the matey misnomer caught him as he made for the exit, past a selection of plastic balls for dispensing liquid detergent, a battered Cluedo, a doll in a dingy knitted dress, and a blur of similar merchandise. Roy went over to the stall where an old acquaintance, Arnie, was doing a brisk trade in Christmas wrapping paper, counterfeit French perfume and watches.

'Like the bins,' said Arnie, indicating Roy's glasses. 'Very high-profile executive whizz-kid.'

'You wouldn't if you could see the magnification of your face,' Roy thought. 'A temporary expedient,' he said. 'I don't think they're quite me.'

'Pathetic, isn't it, what some people have the nerve to try to flog. It's an insult really.' Arnie nodded at the plastic balls, which the vendor was piling into a pyramid, to increase their allure. Roy could only agree.

At home, after telephoning its founder to regret that he must renounce his commitment to Helpline Helpline and hearing that the service had been discontinued, Roy wandered into the back garden. He was sitting hunched on the old swing, kicking a half-buried tambourine sunk under a wodge of once-sprouted birdseed. A relic of Petula's brief post-punk stint as a Salvation Army Songster.

'You look like a garden gnome sitting there.'

'Petula!'

'Hello, Dad. I like the face furniture.'

Roy wrenched off the glasses. He did not want to see Petula through them, and they had misted up besides.

'Pet. My little Pet. Is it really you? Let me look at you.'

He was hugging her so tightly that he could see nothing but smelled the fruit tang of her shiny hair.

'What's in the hutch this time?' she asked. 'Oh, it's a woodpigeon. Hello, Woody. Remember that time we made the Blue Peter bird pudding, Dad? Yuk, it was 'orrible, wasn't it? I was really sick. Still, I suppose we shouldn't have eaten it all ourselves. Mum went spare. Where is she, by the way, church? Shouldn't you be getting the dinner ready? I'll give you a hand. It's freezing out here. Can we go in and have some coffee? And I must put these flowers in water.'

'I can't wait to see your mother's face when she walks in!' said Roy, in the kitchen, groping at the coffee.

'Put your specs on,' advised Petula.

'No, I'm better without them. They're the wrong prescription. They're giving me gyp.'

'Try these.'

Petula took a rhinestone butterfly-winged pair from her bag. 'I don't need them – they're from my fifties period. Found them at a car boot.' she said. Her father's daughter.

They took their coffee into the front room.

'What a tip,' said Petula affectionately. She hooked the glasses over Roy's ears before sweeping aside a box of recycled envelopes and Christmas gift catalogues and sitting down. 'They suit you. How are they?'

84

'Perfect. They're brilliant – might have been made for me. Everything's right in focus. Marvellous! Just the ticket. Let me look at your properly.'

He saw a striking young woman in her thirties, with dark feathered hair and big silver earrings, a bright patterned chunky sweater above black leggings and red boots.

'A sight for sore eyes,' he said.

He studied himself in the mirror through the sparkling unswept frames, and wondered if he might introduce a little tasteful drag into his next entertainment. Then he saw that Petula had arranged a bunch of red carnations in a vase, and forbore to remind her that women in Colombia gave their fingers, even their lives, to the cultivation of those scentless blooms that deck our garage forecourts and corner shops.

Walter Wood passed the window, and shook a fist.

'We had a bit of a misunderstanding – ' Roy started to explain in unhappy embarrassment as the plastic carriers fluttered in the tree outside.

'Miserable old scrote. The thing is, Dad, I want to come home. I've left Barrington. And I've had it up to here with the Witnesses – all that dragging round doorsteps flogging *AWAKE!* and other boring literature, honestly I might just as well have stayed at home with your interminable Flag Days! I was bored to sobs after a fortnight.' She began to sing, to the tune of 'Born to Lose' – 'Bored to sobs, I've lived my life in vain. Every dream has only brought me pain. All my life, I've always been so blue. Bored to sobs, And now I'm bo-ored with you! Not you, Daddy. I know I've disappointed you in the past – I couldn't be cute like Petula Clark or develop an adult larynx like Julie Andrews, but I'll make you proud of me one day.'

'Darling, I've always been so proud – when we went out with you in your little coat, and your doll's pram, and people used to say "she's just like a little doll," and I was as proud as a peacock when your mother brought you down to the bus garage to meet me and I used to show you off to all my mates – and later – '

He had been going to say that he loved her in all her reincarnations and admired her independence of spirit but she cut in defensively with, 'It wasn't easy for me either, you know, you and Mum always being so involved in other people's problems. Sometimes I used to think that you could only relate to someone if they were disabled in some way – sorry, Stumpy, no offence. I had fantasies about wheelchairs and kidney machines. I was in therapy for a while – well it was group I went to – but I had to leave when it transpired that I was the only person there who hadn't been abused by her father. Amazing how it came back to them one by one. God, it was embarrassing – I felt so inferior. I must have been a singularly unattractive kid . . . sorry, Dad, only kidding – I never fancied you either. Joke. Anyway, we'd better rattle those pots and pans, Mum'll be home any minute, even allowing for coffee in the crypt. "What's the recipe today, Jim?" Pigeon pie? Only kidding.'

Tears, laughter and lunch coming to an end, Woody who had joined the party perking up in his box, Friday night's white wine quaffed, Muriel posed the question that Roy had not liked to put.

'Have you had any thoughts of what you might do next, Pet? Careerwise, I mean?'

'Well, I had thought of becoming a therapist. I read somewhere that any screwed-up, pathetic inadequate with no qualifications can set themselves up, so I thought – that's for me! I could use the front room – it would be money for jam. Then again, I thought I might have a baby. Sometime around next March the first seems like as good a time as any . . .'

86

'Oh . . . Pet!'

Petula looked her mother straight in the eye.

'I'm afraid I must warn you, Mummy, that there's a fifty per cent chance that the baby will be dyslexic – it runs in Barrington's family.'

'Oh, the poor little mite! We must do everything – hang on, I've got a leaflet somewhere . . .'

Petula settled back comfortably against the cushion Roy had just placed at her back and held out her cup for more coffee.

Late that afternoon as Roy set out on his bike to fetch some things that Petula had forgotten to bring, he saw that as the light faded the western sky was white above layers of cloud, pale grey and dark grey, barred like cuckoos' wings, and he rode on towards them, the reflective strips on his pedals spinning starry arcs from his feet in the gathering dusk.

The New Year Boy

Every New Year's morning, when they were children, Monica and her brothers woke to find a present under their pillows, some pretty sweeties or a tiny toy or book. The New Year Boy had visited them in the night while they slept. Monica had believed that the New Year Boy, like Father Christmas, came to everybody's house, and it was not until later that she had realised that he had been conjured up by her Scottish grandmother. She saw him as a cherub or cupid or *putto*, the depiction of the baby New Year in a Victorian illustration or scrapbook; magical and rather mischievous, with his beribboned basket of gifts.

There was nothing from the New Year Boy now, of course, – it would have been alarming if there had been – but when Monica woke on New Year's Day and groped for her glasses on the bedside table, she encountered her new diary. She held it in her hand, knowing it to be a jaunty little fellow in a red jacket, with a pencil at the ready like a neatly furled umbrella, or perhaps a sharp, slim, cheerful chap in a flat cap. She smelled the newness of the pristine white pages sandwiched between red covers. As she lay in her large bed, under the billowing quilt and embroidered covers, a big woman in red satin pyjamas, she was at the heart of a kaleidoscope; before she put on her glasses the room was a shifting jumble of colours; a glitter and clutter, dull gold of icons and gilded

88

putti and baby angels who flew about the walls playing musical instruments. Rich dyes and designs of fabric and tapestry glowed in dark jewelled tones.

Sometimes at night, when the old house shifted, a string of a mandolin twanged, a balalaika throbbed a deep note in the darkness, a zither sighed, or the piano started from a doze with a loud crack of contracting wood. Monica taught the piano and the guitar, but she retained her childhood love for the harmonica. It had been love at first sight; the moment she had set eyes on that mouth organ in the music shop window, grinning through wooden teeth set in red tin lips, she had known it was her instrument, for it had her name on it – Harmonica. It could be cheery, it could be melancholy; its merriest jig had undertones of the blues. She could never pass an indigent old busker wheezing out 'Scotland the Brave' without flinging a coin into his cap. Every conceivable joke about her name had been made long ago.

When she opened the heavy curtains the moon still hung like a mistletoe berry in the grey hungover sky; to the east clouds were cold dirty cinders with flashes of unburnt silver foil and orange peel. She turned on the radio and came in on a dirgey Stabat Mater droning echoes of chilly stone in clouds of powdery incense. She switched it off, snatched up a harmonica and treated the people in the upstairs flat to a brisk rendition of 'A Guid New Year Tae Yin An' A' ', and tidied up the kitchen while her bath was running.

The New Year had been seen in with a few friends; Monica had served ginger wine and black bun sent from Scotland, cherry brandy and slivovitch in gold-rimmed glasses painted with fruit. On the last stroke of midnight a first-footer had lurched over the threshold. He was asleep on the sofa now. Monica had forgotten all about him, and the mouth organ and the clatter of dishes had failed to wake him. A first-footer should be dark, and this one had a mat, almost a mattress, of grey-white beard and hair, both wiry and soft like hanks of sheeps' wool caught on a fence. Paperchains susurrated gently in the snores that were drowned by the running of the bath taps, broke from their moorings of sellotape on the ceiling and covered him in pastel coils. Peter, twice divorced, a piano shifter by trade, slept on, sprawled across the inadequate sofa, a huge man in a soft shirt like a Russian peasant's blouse and trousers still tucked into boots. His subconscious was telling him that it was safer to stay asleep because he would not remember if he had carried out his intention to propose to Monica.

Monica, who had been a widow for fifteen years, stood spoiled for choice in a bathroom full of scented soaps, talcs and bubbles. She had no children of her own. She was an Aunt. An Aunt decreed by her nephews and nieces and her pupils, she thought, to be the cleanest aunt in Christendom. Old students sent her photographs of their children, and sometimes the children themselves to teach. Several of her pupils had done well: 'taught by Monica Baker' did not have quite the cachet of 'studied with Nadia Boulanger' but there was her name in the potted biographies in the programme notes, and that gave her great pleasure. She had come upon another twanging out 'The Streets of London' in the underground at Piccadilly Circus.

'You can do better than that, Michael,' she had said, and fined him ten pence, as was her custom, for sloppy practice. Monica adored her brother's children, loved introducing them, saying 'This is my nephew,' or 'These are my nieces,' presenting them like a bouquet of spring flowers. Her favourite niece had given her the diary and Monica thought of her now, as she stepped into fragrant bubbles, her dark hair that smelled so fresh, of sun and wind and faintly of the sea. She wondered if her own hair had had that perfume, when she was young, with her young husband. This morning she would walk in the park, as she did every New Year's Day, and remember him. He had died on the first day of the year, when the scent of hyacinths, so blue and pure and piercing, had filled this flat.

As she padded back to the bedroom in her robe to dress, she noticed for the first time how stale and nicotine smelling was the air. She must open all the windows, especially in the sitting room, and fumigate the place before she went out. She had an engagement that afternoon, playing the piano at a New Year party at a nearby retirement home, although it was a mystery to her why previously sane people should exhibit, as a symptom of geriatric decline, a sudden desire to play bingo and sing songs from the Boer War. She would take along a harmonica and try them with a few riffs of Dylan and Donovan. There would be cake and paper cups of sherry. Last year, when pressed to imbibe the dark sweet liquid she had conceded with, 'Oh, just a thimbleful, thank you, I insist . . .'

The young Filipino nurse had looked bemused and disappeared, returning ten minutes later with a battered silver thimble, into which she solemnly dribbled three drops of sherry. This year Monica resolved to accept her paper cup with good grace and leave it undrunk on the top of the tone-deaf piano.

Dressed in magenta and mazarine blue, Monica strode in her green boots into the sitting room, and screamed. Peter jumped to his feet, smacked in the eye by a walking hangover. A black cigarette fell from his lips to the carpet. He ground it out with his boot. Monica stamped her foot in its green boot. He watched with dull interest; he had never seen anybody stamp her foot in rage before. Had he or hadn't he asked her to be his wife? He thought she

91

might be a bit – colourful – to face first thing every morning. Her eyes were framed in harlequin rims.

'You're looking very – bright,' he said. 'Oh, I almost forgot, I brought you something last night. A New Year present, but I didn't get round to giving it to you.'

He fished in the pocket of his army-surplus greatcoat which was slumped in a corner, and pulled out an empty vodka bottle. He dropped it and it rolled away, a glass cossack hopelessly drunk on parade. He drew something from another pocket.

'Happy New Year.'

It was a broken blue hyacinth in a pot.

Monica snatched it, rushed over to the window, and flung it out.

'I'm going for a walk!'

Pausing only to slash a scarlet lipstick across her mouth, throw on a necklace of heavy amber and a viridian poncho, she dashed out of the front door. Peter lumbered after her, struggling into his coat.

'Something I said?' he panted. 'The hyacinth? I'll get you another . . .'

A drizzling rain was making the park very green. Monica stalked in tears past the bench in the bare pergola where she had intended to sit holding the hand of her husband's ghost. Peter pounded along beside her.

'Monica, wait! About last night, did I . . .?'

'Go away. Please. I need to be alone with my thoughts, I – I've got a professional engagement this afternoon.'

'A gig?'

'An engagement. I don't play gigs. I'm an artiste.' Thirty years ago she had played a summer season at the Gaiety Theatre, Ayr, billed as the Nairn Nightingale, accompanying herself on the concertina, with the Jinty McShane Dancers, game old birds in tartan tutus, pirouetting behind her.

A squirrel watched them from a branch now.

92

'I'm sorry, I've nothing for you,' said Monica.

She remembered the warm gingerbread boys with melting icing buttons that she made for her pupils. As she spoke, an old black bicycle wobbled round the corner, a small boy at the pedals, and a panting father clutching the saddle from behind to steady him. They careened to an ungainly halt.

'Excuse me,' Peter said. He unwound the long scarf from the astonished and perspiring, but too puffed-out to resist, father's neck and looped it round the boy's waist, putting the two ends in the father's hands.

'Try it like this,' he said. 'It never fails.' They got the bike upright and Peter muttered in the father's ear, 'The trick is knowing when to let go.'

As father, bicycle and boy riding high and confident disappeared into a green blur, Monica had to wipe her glasses, both sides of the lenses, and as she replaced them she saw Peter's terrible mat of hair and beard spangled with silver drizzle, and perceived him in that second as a viable proposition. Perhaps ... she visualised a pair of shears – there was enough of it to stuff a cushion – and remembered an electric razor of her husband's that she had kept, an obsolete old Remington with twin heads of meshed steel. Peter, meanwhile, had found an irritating bit of walnut shell stuck in a tooth, and recalled that her books were double-parked on her shelves. There would be no room for his own.

'Peter ...'

He looked at her; a tough nut to crack, an obdurate Brazil, a tightly closed pistachio. He had had a narrow escape. 'I'll leave you to your thoughts,' he said, and left her on the path.

Later, at home that evening, regretting the cup of sherry to which she had succumbed at the elderly resident's party, Monica thought about the electric razor. Suppose she had taken it from its case and blown away a speck of hair, a tiny particle of him which she had; lost for ever. The old-fashioned radiator rumbled, the wind whimpered in the chimney, and a drift of soot pattered the paper fan in the fireplace. She settled comfortably, a magpie in a big glittery nest, with room to stretch her wings. She reached for her diary and began entering her name and address with faint anticipation. All those white pages, waiting to be filled.

Shinty

In the autumn the little girls of the Vineyard school would build fragile mansions from the fallen leaves in the shrubbery. The houses had no roofs except the laurels, rhododendrons and firs above but the grandest of them boasted walls three or four feet high and many rooms. The groundplans were scratched with sticks on the sandy soil and marked out with foundations gathered from the deciduous drifts of oak, sweet chestnut leaves, acorns, beech mast and pine needles. Wind, rain or spiteful shoes could demolish in seconds the work of many playtimes. The Vineyard was an ordinary primary school in a Kent town but it was privileged in its building, a Georgian house, and took only girls.

The smell of damp sand and cold leaves came back to Margaret so vividly as she read the advertisement in the paper that forty years dissolved and she might have been in 'the shrubs' with her greatest treasure, an ostrich egg, crushed to chips of yellowish white shell in her hands. Chestnut cases picked her fingers, the bitter taste of flat pale unripened fruit was in her mouth, and she remembered a girl called Jean Widdoes, who had scraped together a hovel in the dankest corner of the shrubs, where she dwelt alone in the long dinner hour.

Ronnie Sharples Reads From Her
Latest Best Seller

Flowers of Evil
At Dorothy's Bookshop, Flitcroft Court,
Charing Cross Road
Thursday 23 September 7.00
Ring to Reserve Signed Copies
Glass Of Wine Or Ale
Women Only

Veronica Sharples, her old classmate, whose books automatically shot straight into the number one slot of the Alternative Best Sellers.

Margaret rang Suzy at once, at work. They had been best friends at seven and were best friends still. Suzy, who had always ended up with at least ten extra stitches on her knitting, now had her own computer graphics company. When the class had started their tea cosies, Veronica, given first choice, had picked 'Camel and nigger, please Mrs Lambie.' Her words had stayed with Margaret all these years. All that remained when it came to Margaret's turn was dull orange and bottle green; the crimson lake and sea-green knitted fluted jelly that she had envisaged for as long as it took to distribute the wool, that would transform their broken-spouted teapot, was not to be; in fact it turned into a kettle-holder full of holes. She could hear Mrs Lambie's voice now, striking terror along the desks in needlework:

'Unpick it!' 'Unpick it!' 'Unpick it!' 'That's a lovely little run-and-fell seam, Veronica. You're developing into quite a nice little needlewoman.' No terror in adult life would match that of double needlework with Mrs Lambie.

'Are you sure we're ready for this?' Suzy asked. 'I mean, Veronica Sharples . . . will we have to have our bodies pierced to pass ourselves off as fans? There's no way I'm paying out good money to feed her monstrous ego and you know her books are quite unreadable. Dennis Wheatley and The Girls of the Chalet School meet the Clan of the Cave Bear at The Well of Loneliness – no thanks. What would be the point of going? She'd only think we were impressed.'

'This is the point,' said Margaret, 'we'll go in disguise. Surely you don't imagine she'd remember us anyway? Be in the Beaujolais at six on Thursday, and we can fortify ourselves for the fray. Bring your shinty stick.'

She put the phone down without hearing Suzy's whine of 'It'll be just like school, everybody standing round watching Veronica showing off,' but realised she was humming 'The Deadwood Stage' and was transported back to the washbasins, as the lavatories at the Vineyard were known, where Veronica leaped on to a toilet seat, breaking it, in her imitation of Calamity Jane. Whip crack away, whip crack away, whip crack away! 'Do the "Dying swan", Veronica,' someone begged, and Veronica closed her eyes, assumed a doleful expression, clasped her hands in a coronet above her head, and died on the tiled floor, as a coterie of clumsy cygnets waited in the wings for tuition in the art of the arabesque.

Veronica was the arbiter of fashion and her dress code was as immutable as her social strictures. Jean 'Fish-Face' Widdoes, whose mother by cruel chance was a widow, who worked in a chip shop, had once turned up, horror of horrors, in a knitted pixie-hood, and on another occasion in pink ankle socks edged with a blue stripe. 'Baby's socks, 1/11 in Woolworths' pronounced Veronica, who had spotted them at once. 'Oh, look, your legs are going all blotchy to match your socks.' It was extremely bad form, and dangerous, to admit to any home life – especially if like Linda Wells, you had a brother who was mental. To bring to the classroom a faint reminder of the previous night's fried food was a serious offence, and one which did not endear Jean to the teachers either, although they did not grasp their noses at her approach, as the girls did. The Dolphin Fish Bar in Arbutus Road was a hundred yards downhill from the swimming baths, and on Saturdays, when Jean helped in the shop, there was always the threat that Veronica and her pals would appear in the queue, blue-lipped and red-eyed, reeking of chlorine, sleek-haired mobsters in cotton frocks and cardigans. Jean paid protection in extra chips and free pickled eggs. Once, when Margaret was in the Dolphin with her own mother, she heard Jean's mother suggesting that Jean might like to go swimming with her friends sometimes instead of serving in the shop. Jean shook her head so vehemently that the big white turban she wore slipped right down over her face. 'Oh, go on, Jeannie, plee-ease, be a sport, we'll call for you tomorrow,' pleaded Veronica, so eloquently that Jean was persuaded that she would not be *the* sport. Foolish little Fish-Face, forgetting about the diving board as she trotted along with her costume rolled in her towel. 'It looks like a fish, it smells like a fish, but it sure don't swim like a fish,' Veronica summed it up.

'Why don't you like Jean?' somebody challenged Veronica one day.

'Because she's got a big conk and she's smelly.'

When Margaret told Suzy to arm herself with her shinty stick for the reading, she was making a reference to the half-moon-shaped scar above Suzy's ankle, the memory of a wound inflicted when Veronica had tripped her up, making her fall on the sharp-edged tin that held the shinty balls. For reasons best known to Miss Short who taught Hygiene and PT, and presumably with the headmistress, Miss Barnard's approval, the Vineyard girls played shinty rather than hockey. Perhaps the smaller sticks made the playing field look larger. There was no gymnasium, and wet games and PT lessons took place in the cloakrooms. Miss Short was particularly fond of an activity called 'duckwalking' wherein the girls had to

98

crook their arms into wings and waddle at speed round the narrow benches and pegs hung with coats and shoe-bags. Quacking was forbidden. If there had been a Junior Olympic Duckwalking event, Veronica would have walked it, with her bony wings pumping from her blind-ing white vest – somebody's mum always used Persil – and jaunty little navy blue bottom jerking from side to side over speedy plimsoles as she lapped the field. Veron-ica was Miss Short's pet duckling and Miss Short turned a blind eye to a wing winding a rival, as she did to wet netballs smacking an opponent's face or knees grazing asphalt in a heavy fall; but it was at shinty that Veronica really shone, her own sharp shins, the blade bone of her nose, honed to a finer point than Jean's despised conk, cutting a swathe through the opposing team, although she was never a team player.

After speaking to Suzy, Margaret decided that the years that had passed since Veronica had seen her old schoolmates would provide sufficient disguise, and besides, Veronica had not watched them, as they had watched her, on the television, strutting her stuff on *01 For London*. As is customary on that programme, the interview took place in a restaurant of the guest's choice, and Veronica had opted for Bob's Eel and Pie House, an establishment in Smithfield which had repulsed trendi-ness, where, elbows on the formica table top, mouth full of jelly, she had chomped on working-class solidarity while charting her progress from the rural and cultural poverty of her childhood to her present cult status. All had gone swimmingly until the interviewer had asked, in his affable Scottish way, 'Are ye no slumming it a wee bit the night though, Ronnie? I mean to say, rumour has it that you have your own special table in the Groucho, where you're to be found most evenings?'

The camera lingered on him as eels, mash, liquor and peas slid down his face from the plate upturned on his head, and then pursued Veronica as she wrenched open the door of the Ronniemobile parked outside and was chauffeused away at speed.

Margaret was no longer the plump child she had been when 'Twice round the gasworks, once round the Maggot' had been Veronica's estimation of her size, but as she got ready for the evening's entertainment, her dress felt a little tight. How typical of Veronica to make her put on weight today. 'Pooh! can anybody smell gas?' was Veronica's taunt when Margaret was out of favour. Home was number 5 Gasworks Cottages. Suzy lived in a tiny village, just a street with a shop, a pub and a church, a farm, a scattering of villas and cottages and a crescent of new council houses. She came to school on the bus.

When Margaret, dressed as herself, Margaret Jones, who had recently celebrated her silver wedding, mother of four grown-up children, regional director of a large housing association, arrived at the Beaujolais, she saw a black fedora waving at her through the smoke of the crowded room. Suzy had got herself up as a gangster in a wasp-waisted pinstripe suit, and as Margaret squeezed on to the chair she had managed to reserve, she flashed open her jacket to show the butt of a gun poking from her inside pocket.

'I was going to get a violin case but I thought it would be a bit obvious,' she said.

'Mmm. That's *so* much more subtle. Sorry I'm late, there's been a bomb scare at Charing Cross and half the Strand's closed off. Bloody security alerts, it's probably just some jerk of a commuter who left his briefcase on the concourse.' She poured herself a glass of wine from the bottle on the table.

'Sweet of you to save some for me. Cheers. That thing in your pocket is a toy, I hope?'

'Realistic, though, eh? What happened to your disguise, and where's your shinty stick?'

100

'Funnily enough, I couldn't find it – possibly because Veronica Sharples was the only girl who had her own shinty stick – and unbeknownst to you, there is a liberty bodice with rubber buttons concealed beneath this workaday print. I've come as Jean Widdoes.' She had just remembered how Jean Widdoes had been the only girl in the school, perhaps the last girl in the world, to wear one of those obsolete padded vests.

'Jean Widdoes is dead,' said Suzy.

'What? I don't believe you. When? Why didn't you tell me?'

'Sorry. It was while you were in France in the spring. My mother sent me a cutting from the local paper. Her car was hit by a train on a level crossing. It was an open verdict. I didn't send it on to you because you had enough troubles of your own, and then I suppose I just blocked it out. Couldn't bear to think about it.'

'It doesn't bear thinking about.'

She wished she had not brought up the liberty bodice. PT lessons had been made hell on its account until Jean learned to take it off beforehand and hide it in her shoebag.

'Remember that awful time her mother dragged her screaming into assembly and she was clinging to her in hysterics, and Miss Barnard said, 'I still have my cane, Jean.'?

'Yes – they knew how to cure school phobia in them days – I wish we weren't doing this,' Margaret said. 'Shall we just go and have something to eat instead? It doesn't seem so amusing now, and you could do with some blotting paper.'

'What, and waste this suit?'

Margaret wished herself miles away from bodies and braying laughter, and fumes of wine, smoke and charcuterie, in the heart of the Kent they had shared, a tumbledown place of old yellow-lichened red brick, sagging garden walls held up by old man's beard, old rabbit hutches and chicken runs, virginia creeper and apples and rosehips against blue autumn sky, dark lacy cabbages, quinces and wasps, the bittersweet smell of hops.

But there was Legs Diamond waving two tickets at her and saying, 'I made a special trip at lunchtime to get them. There are bound to be coachloads of Ronnie's little fans.'

She took her ticket, drained her glass, stubbed out her cigarette and squeezed herself out of her chair to follow her friend.

'There she is!' Suzy clutched Margaret's arm outside the shop, whose window was dominated by a blown-up photograph of Ronnie surrounded by pyramids of her books. 'No it isn't, it's a clone. My God, there are hundreds of them. Surrounded by Ronnie Sharples Wannabees, what a terrifying prospect. Do you think we'll be all right?'

'No,' said Margaret.

'It was your idea, remember. Another nice mess you've got me into . . .'

As that could not be denied there was nothing to say. Miss Barnard's voice came faintly through the ether, 'Margaret Adams, you are a bad influence and you, Susan Smithers, are weak and easily led. Together you make a deplorable pair. I am separating you for the rest of the term.'

Apart from the chums, as Margaret christened herself and Suzy grimly, the audience was composed of young women and girls with short hair gelled back from their foreheads, dressed in polo shirts tucked into knee-length khaki shorts fastened with snake belts.

'Gott in Himmel! The Hitler Youth!' whispered Suzy.

'They've all copied exactly what she was wearing on *01 For London*! What must it be like to have a following like that? The Michael Jackson of literature.' Margaret whis-

102

pered back, thinking that they looked like a troop of Boy Scouts that Baden-Powell wouldn't have touched with a tent-pole. Camp as a row of tents. Then she recalled Veronica, sleek-haired after the swimming baths, except that she had worn a cotton frock in those days. Each of the clones carried a copy of Ronnie's latest book, *Flowers of Evil*, and some of them carried six-packs of Thackray's Old Peculiar Ale.

'Original title . . .' Margaret commented, of the book.

A shop assistant was trying to hold the door open just wide enough for several of the scouts to evict an old wino woman who had managed to infiltrate, while repelling latecomers at the same time.

'So much for sisterhood,' as Suzy remarked.

Dorothy, the bookshop's owner, was looking worriedly at her watch. Ronnie Sharples had a reputation for unpredictability.

'She'll be here,' her friend and business partner was reassuring her, 'Her girlfriend was on the phone again only an hour ago to confirm we'd got the right ale in.'

'Did you reassure her that the dumb duck who shelved *Wicca and Willow* with the Craft Books was sacked on the spot as soon as she confessed?'

If only Ronnie's sidekick hadn't spotted it when she was in checking the window display. The event had almost been cancelled.

A small table held a jug of water, a bottle of red wine, half-empty, a similar bottle of white, some plastic cups, and a crate of Thackray's Old Peculiar, the extra-strong Northern ale which was all that Ronnie, despising the Kentish hopfields of her youth, would drink. More cans were stacked below.

'Our Ronnie was always heavily into uniforms, wasn't she?' said Suzy, as she paid for two cups of wine. Margaret felt a pang of shame remembering how she had cajoled her parents into buying a new blazer that they could ill

103

afford. There was a Vineyard uniform of blue blazer, gymslip, white blouse and blue and white striped tie, but it was optional; a few girls, like Margaret whose was second-hand, wore blazers but that was as far as it went. Until the arrival of Veronica in the middle of the third year, in the full rig or fig. She even sported a blue pancake, with a badge. The force of Veronica's personality was such that Easterfield's the High Street Outfitters enjoyed an unprecedented boom, and the more berets there were on heads meant, to Veronica and the gang she had formed at once, the more berets to toss into trees and pull down over people's eyes. Strange though that she, the proponent of the Windsor knot in the school tie that was such a useful garotte, should have made Miss Harvey, who wore a collar and necktie with her tailored coat and skirt, the target of her scorn.

'Old Ma Harvey looks a right twerp in that tie,' Veronica decreed, and it was so. Margaret, who loved Miss Harvey and yearned for a tweed or tartan tie, cried for Miss Harvey secretly in the washbasins. Her heart bled for Miss Harvey, knotting her tie in the mirror in the morning, sitting on her desk, swinging her legs as she read them *The Kon-Tiki Expedition*, unaware that she had been diminished by Veronica calling her a right twerp. Veronica put up her hand.

'How did they go to the toilet, Miss Harvey?'

The class was shocked at the rudeness and audacity of Veronica's question, but Miss Harvey laughed like the good sport she was. Margaret longed for brogues like Miss Harvey's too, shiny brown and punched with interesting patterns of holes. 'Old Ma Harvey,' indeed. Veronica and her gang knew nothing of the real Miss Harvey.

'I bet she wears trousers at home,' Margaret told Suzy. 'She only has to wear a skirt at school because it's the law.' Suzy agreed. They had lurked outside Miss Harvey's house one afternoon in the holidays in the hope of seeing

104

her but a cross old lady in gardening trousers had advanced on them with a trowel as they passed the gate of Heronsmere Cottage for the tenth time, and they had run away. Cycling home from Miss Harvey's village, they wondered how someone as nice as Miss Harvey could have such a grumpy old mother.

'Remember how Veronica got the Grammar uniform before we'd even sat the scholarship?' Margaret asked, as they waited for her to appear.

'And wore it on Saturdays!'

'If only she hadn't passed . . .'

'Jean Widdoes passed too didn't she? But she didn't go, for some reason.'

'Do you think I should tell them that Ronnie didn't turn up as guest speaker at the Sevenoaks Soroptimists?' Suzy was saying as the audience grew restive on its seats, when the heavy glass door crashed open, flattening the assistant against a bookcase.

Twin Tontons Macoutes in mirror sunglasses swung in, followed by Ronnie, elfin in white T-shirt and black jeans. Scattered applause, whistles and disappointed sighs came from her fans, in their shorts and polo shirts. Sidling in as the door banged shut came a tall, drooping young woman in limp viscose, with long pale hair pushed behind her ears. Mog, Ronnie's latest partner and general factotum. Rumour had it that she had been bought as a slave in Camden Market. The crocodile Kelly bag that Mog carried suggested that Ronnie had tried to make something of her, but Quality Seconds had prevailed. A plaster was coming unstuck from one of her heels where her sandals had rubbed blisters.

'It's guts for garters time if we get clamped again,' were the first words the faithful heard from their idol, and Mog's muttered reference to a disabled sticker was lost as she ripped the tab from the can of Thackray's handed to her by the genuflecting Dorothy, and gave it to Ronnie.

'I think we should make a start as soon as you're ready,' Dorothy suggested timidly, 'We are running a tad late . . . if you don't mind. I'll just give brief introduction . . .'

'A tad late?' Ronnie interrupted her. 'Half of bloody London's closed off. Think yourself lucky we're here at all.'

'Oh, we do, Ronnie. We do.'

'Ronnie needs no introduction,' put in Mog in a monotone as flat as her face.

'Shut up, Mog or I'll cancel the cheque for your assertiveness class.'

Ronnie gave Mog an affectionate nudge which sprayed Old Peculiar over her frock. Mog gazed down on her adoringly and gratefully at this public display of intimacy. Margaret whispered into Suzy's ear a poem they had learned in school:

> 'Rufty and Tufty were two little elves
> They lived in a hollow tree . . .
> Rufty was clever and kept the accounts
> While Tufty preferred to do cooking.
> He could bake a cake without a mistake,
> And eat it when no one was looking!'

'It's like the black hole of Calcutta in here. Haven't you got any air conditioning?' Ronnie demanded and at once a Tonton Macoute switched on the electric fan that stood by the till sending a whirlwind of leaflets into the front row of the audience, as the police and ambulance sirens drowned Dorothy's apologies as she scrambled after the papers. Mog, flanked by the bodyguards, was seated in the front row, after reassurances that a thorough search of the premises for incendiary devices had been made, as

106

ordered, earlier. Ronnie suspected that she was a prime target.

'It would be like the IRA's biggest coup ever if they got Ronnie,' Mog explained. 'We have to be like constantly vigilant. Security's a real hassle.'

Dorothy, stained with shyness at the ordeal of public speaking, was motioning for silence in the ranks.

'OK, OK, let's 'ave a bit of 'ush. Right, well, we're really honoured to have with us tonight someone who needs no introduction from me. Dorothy's is proud and privileged to welcome the writer who has been called variously 'the lodestar of lesbian literature' and the 'Anne Hathaway de nos jours'. So please put your hands together in a great big Dorothy's welcome for your own, your very own, RONNIE SHARPLES!!'

Suzy gave Margaret a questioning nudge under cover of the catcalls and whistles that broke out, as Dorothy sat down heavily after her lapse into the persona she had assumed for her role as mistress of ceremony at the ill-starred Old Tyme Varieties at the Drill Hall one Christmas.

'Don't tell me you haven't read *Dyke Lady of The Sonnets*, or *Second Best Bard*, which proves Anne Hathaway wrote the plays,' Margaret replied.

'Hi gang.' Ronnie waited for silence to follow the return of her greeting, then snatched up the copy of *Flowers of Evil* that lay, bristling with bookmarks, in Mog's ample lap. She opened the book, and took a swig from her can.

'Hope you've all bought a copy, or three . . .'

Only two pairs of hands were still as a flock of books rose and flapped their pages in the air.

'Right then, we can all go home . . .'

Through the laughter came the sound of the door rattling and the Tonton Macoute posted there shouting, 'Can't you read, dickhead? It says Wimmin Only!' She held the bulging door, calling over her shoulder, 'Boss, some wanker says he's your dad!'

'Oh, for fuck's sake! Deal with it, Mog. Get rid of him. Take the bloody diary and see if I've got a window after Christmas. Just do it, you great waste of space!' Ronnie's lips were thin bloodless scars of fury in her livid face. The front row squirmed in their seats. Before Mog made it to the door the gatecrasher disappeared and a megaphone was thrust in, and the bouncer stepped back to admit a uniformed policeman.

'Nobody is to leave the building until the police give clearance that it is safe to do so,' he said, and backed out, pulling the door closed behind him. Yellow official tape sealed them in. Ronnie ran to the door, dragging it open.

'What is this, a police state, now?'

She was thrust courteously but ignominiously back inside as an explosion down the road erupted ale from cans and hurled books to the floor.

'Bye bye, Daddy. It was nice knowing you,' Ronnie attempted to retrieve lost face. 'Where d'you think you're going, Madam?' She grabbed Mog by the hair.

'People may be hurt, Ronnie. I've got my first-aid badge, I must go.'

'They need paramedics not bloody Brownies, you dip-stick!' But Mog twisted free, leaving a hank of pale hair wound round Ronnie's fingers, and escaped.

'You're fired! And I want that bloody ring back!'

A cluster of clones surrounded Ronnie, comforting, placating, tacitly offering themselves as replacements. She thrust them aside.

'Where's the loo in this dump? I need some space.'

'This way Ronnie, I'll show you,' Dorothy was saying soothingly, but Ronnie pushed past her and strode to the back of the shop and wrenched open a door. When it proved to be a cupboard holding cleaning materials, she shut herself in anyway, defying anybody to recognise a cliché of farce, sharing her space with a vileda mop and bucket.

Margaret turned to Suzy, and saw that she was crying.

'Her father was such a nice man,' she sobbed. 'He was really good fun. Remember when he bought us all ice-cream after the pageant, the one when Ronnie was Elizabeth the First, and we were scullions?' She scrubbed at her eyes with a tissue. 'Only that pathetic Mog had the guts to do anything.'

'Look, the explosion was miles away, probably right down in Trafalgar Square. It sounded pretty feeble anyway, a small incendiary device. There's no way Mr Sharples could have been in it.'

Her own feelings of guilt at not having done as Mog had done, and uselessness, made her voice impatient. Instinct told her that people were not bleeding and dying yards away, but how could she be sure?

The cupboard door opened and Ronnie emerged, clinging to the mop handle looking ill.

'It's Mrs Mop, the Cockney Treasure,' said Margaret, trying to make Suzy laugh.

'What's *your* problem?' said a voice behind her.

Margaret turned, her smile withered by the hate on the face that was saying, 'Sitting there sniggering in your Laura Ashley frigging frock. I suppose it offends your middle-class mores that someone like Ronnie should be a working-class gay icon. Some people just can't stand to see anybody from the wrong background succeed. Why don't you piss off back to Hampstead, Lipstick Lesbian, and take your fashion victim girlfriend with you?'

'It isn't Laura Ashley,' was all that Margaret could say. She was frightened, expecting a fist in her face. She turned round again, trembling, but Suzy had slewed round indignantly.

'Working class? You've got to be joking. If you believe that you'll believe any of Ronnie's hype and lies. Veronica

Sharples was the first girl in our class to have a patio, *and* the first to have a car, one of those green jobs with woodwork, *and, and* she went on holiday to the Costa del Sol before it was even invented, so don't give me that underprivileged crap. *And* you should have seen her lunch – a big Oxo tin crammed with sandwiches, and that was just for playtime.'

'Leave it, Suze,' said Margaret.

'Leave it, Suze,' her accuser imitated her.

'*And* your working-class icon went to Cambridge.'

'So what?'

'So nothing, except Veronica Sharples is a fraud as well as a lousy writer. *And* they had their own chalet at Camber Sands!'

Margaret heard Veronica's childish voice pipe, 'Anyway, *we've* got a vestibule!' and her own defiant retort 'Well my dad's getting us one tomorrow, so there!'

She pulled Suzy to her feet. 'Come on, we might as well get a drink, as we seem to be stuck here for the duration. Everybody else is helping herself.'

A can of Thackray's was preferable to a necktie party, she decided, noting the mirror shades of a Macoute reflecting the argument, even though Old Peculiar might not mix with the wine Suzy had drunk earlier.

'I suddenly realised I – I mean, all of us – might have been killed,' they heard Ronnie say. 'Somebody better deal with that bucket in there.'

As they stood apart in a corner, drinking their ale, Margaret thought about her ostrich egg. When her father had brought it home from a Toc H jumble sale, she had begged to be allowed to take it to school. Her mother had relented at last, against her better judgement. Margaret had been standing in the playground, the centre of an admiring circle, holding the big, frail, miraculous thing, when Veronica had come up behind her and grabbed

Margaret's hands and clapped them together shattering the shell,

'Now look what you've been and gone and done! Oh' Veronica crowed 'dear what a pity never mind. What will Mummy say now? Boo hoo.'

That was what she always said when she made somebody cry: Oh dear what a pity never mind. But why had she wanted to make other children cry? Was it in rehearsal for her life as a writer, a testing of her power to move to tears? If so, art had failed to imitate life. Perhaps, then, Veronica had no choice, her character as predetermined as the blade of her nose. Margaret pictured a phrenologist's porcelain head with bulging prominences marked Spite, Ambition, Envy, and a tiny section just big enough to contain the blurred word Talent.

'There's something I never told you,' Suzy said.

'Let me guess, you kissed Veronica in the bike shed?'

'I was her best friend for a day.'

'What? You traitor! how could you?' Her childhood was cracking like eggshell.

'No, she made me, it was awful. It was a Sunday and she just suddenly appeared at the top of our lane, and I was playing with that little girl Doreen, she was only about four, with her doll's pram, and I was wearing my mum's white peep-toes and one of her old dance frocks. Veronica said she'd tell everybody at school that I played with dollies if I wouldn't be her best friend. And the worst thing was, Keith Maxfield shouted out 'Oo's that queer gink?' as she came down the lane, no, the worst thing was, my mother, mistaking her for a nice little school friend, invited her to tea. She pushed my baby sister down the stairs, accidentally on purpose. When I was walking her back to the bus stop the cows came down the lane and Veronica said, 'I do pity you, Suzy, living in all this cows' muck.'

'Oh dear what a pity never mind.'

'And she tried to hang my teddy from the apple tree with elastic . . .'

'This catalogue of crimes only makes your perfidy more indefensible. Why didn't you tell me?'

'I was going to – you must remember how scary she was – and anyway, on the Monday, that new girl Madeleine came, and Veronica forgot all about me. Natch. I was only ten, Margaret . . .'

'Only obeying orders, you mean.'

A crash of glass might have been a damaged window of an adjacent shop leaving its moorings, or the sound of someone in a glass house throwing stones. As people converged on Dorothy's window to see what was happening in the street, her own little jagged lump of guilt began to cut. There was a girl named Angela Billings who had a slight speech impediment. One playtime stumbling over her words, Margaret had produced an accidental approximation to Angela's diction.

'Hey, listen, Margaret's super at taking-off Angela Billings! Go on, Margaret, do it again!' called Ronnie.

Shamefaced after feeble protestations, Margaret had. And again, enjoying the brief warmth of Veronica's friends' laughter, Veronica's arm round her shoulder.

'She got bitten by a horse fly,' Suzy was saying, 'and she said it would be my fault if it went septic and she had to have her leg off. I was sick with fear.'

Time passed. Dorothy looked increasingly desperate as people mulled aimlessly around her. Ronnie looked at her watch, as if she had another appointment.

'This is getting ridiculous. Get Scotland Yard or the Bomb Squad on the phone,' she commanded. 'They've no right to keep us cooped up in here like a load of bloody Bosnians under fire. Where's that Little Hitler with the loud hailer?'

'History was always Veronica's strong point,' said Suzy,

112

loud enough for Ronnie to whirl round and demand, 'Do I know you?'

'Torture, wasn't it, that really turned you on? Medieval punishments? An early interest that was to bear fruit in your mature work. No, you don't know me. But I wonder if you'd do me the honour of signing this book for me?' She pulled a book off a shelf. Ronnie struck it away contemptuously.

'Are you out of your trees? Why should I sign somebody else's book? I don't even *read* other people's books!'

'Is it? Oh dear what a pity never mind, an easy mistake . . .'

'The Old Bill wasn't very helpful, Boss,' reported a twin.

'Look, Ronnie, in the circumstances, I'm prepared to double your fee – if you'll just give us a short reading . . . we're running out of booze . . .' Dorothy pleaded, as fans, following Suzy's lead, surrounded Ronnie waving books and pens.

As Margaret, her second can of Thackray's half-drunk, watched them, the scene dissolved into the washbasins where a little girl executed an arabesque against the snowlight of a winter afternoon. She was just a child, she thought, we were all only children. A muzzy mellow maternal benevolence suffused her, absolving her of her betrayal of Angela Billings; far away, made tiny by the perspective of the years, Ronnie danced, as fragile and guiltless as a ballerina pirouetting atop a musical jewel casket to a tinkling tune. Margaret turned to Suzy, her eyes bright with unshed tears.

'School,' she told her, 'is a place for learning – '

'No! You don't say! I'd never have known.'

'No, I mean – lessons in life. About ourselves, our limits and weaknesses, and how to overcome them . . .'

'No wonder they call this stuff Old Peculiar. And I thought you flunked that Open University Philosophy course . . .'

113

Margaret had to swallow her tears, just as if someone had given her the good playground pinch she had been tempted to inflict on her friend.

'What I'm trying to say is – Veronica can't be held responsible for Jean's suicide.'

'Nobody suggested she could, just because she ruined the childhood of a short and presumably unhappy life. "Every child has the right to be happy," that's what you've told me often enough, isn't it? Mummy?'

Margaret plonked down her drink, and made towards Ronnie, bursting with something, she didn't know that, that she had to say to her.

Ronnie was berating an abject Dorothy:

'Look, there's no way I'm giving a reading of any kind whatsoever at this shambles. The whole thing's a monumental cockup. You can give me a cheque for three, no make it four, times what we agreed, to compensate for my time and mental trauma and' – she looked round for something to add to the bill – 'and the break-up of my relationship!'

'You aren't too complimentary about her thighs here,' Suzy's voice was loud in the respectful silence cast by the reference to the departed Mog. She had got hold of a copy of *Flowers of Evil* and was stabbing her finger at the opening line.

Ronnie's face was white, the bone in her nose razor sharp, and two crimson patches blazed on her cheeks. Margaret knew that look, that dangerous painted doll face: something was about to get broken; a house of leaves kicked to pieces.

'Veronica,' she said; as Ronnie ripped the cloth from the table and empties, the bottles and plastic cups and a jug of water crashed to the floor.

'How dare you make remarks about my lover's thighs!' she shouted at Suzy. 'I do know you – you were at school with me! I know who you are, bitch, you're that Fish-Face

114

creature aren't you? Who the hell let you in here to wreck my reading? My God, you've got a nerve! Get her out of here!'

The Tontons Macoute were moving towards Suzy as Ronnie yelled, 'Still stink of chips do you Fish-Face? Go on, give us a pickled egg!' The macoutes closed in on Suzy. One of them twisted her arm behind her back.

'*And* there was something fishy about your mother! Wasn't she the local tart or something?'

Margaret grabbed at the other bodyguard's arm, her fingers slipping in slick sweat, and was shrugged contemptuously off, bounced against a bookshelf.

'Freeze! Hold it right there!' Suzy had scrabbled the gun from her pocket with her free hand and had it trained on Ronnie's head. Her attacker dropped her arm and stepped away.

'It's only a gun, you wimps!' Ronnie shrieked, 'Get it off her!'

The entire audience, but for Margaret, and the bodyguards oozed backwards against the windows and the sealed door.

'Do something! Kill her, put her in hospital! You're all pathetic, you're all fired, the lot of you! I forbid you to so much as open one of my books as long as you live! Give them all back!'

'Cool it, Veronica,' said Suzy. 'You know what this reminds me of? A wet PT lesson in the cloakroom. Shame we can't get out on the shinty field and hack each other's shins, isn't it? Still, never mind. Forgotten your plimsoles again, have you, or perhaps the truth is that you don't in fact possess any plimsoles? Take a pair out of the school box then, quick sharp – those khaki ones with no laces. Vests and knickers, everybody, and you can take off that ridiculous liberty bodice, Jean Widdoes, I don't care if your mother does say you've got a weak chest, it's your

115

weak brain that concerns *me*. Buck up, you're like a lot of old ladies!'

A sycophantic titter came from the back. Suzy crossed the room and pressed the gun behind Ronnie's ear. She addressed the paralysed fans.

'Right, form two teams, Reds and Greens, quick sharp! Margaret, give out the bands!'

Margaret almost stepped forward to distribute the rough red and green hessian bands but realised she was in a bookshop where Suzy, with a gun, was imitating Miss Short. However, the fans and Tontons were scrambling into two untidy lines, fighting not to be at the front. A couple of cravens had stripped to vests and knickers.

'Dorothy, you're Green Captain. You, Veronica, can be Captain of the Reds. Where's my whistle?'

'Here, miss, you can use mine.'

A silver whistle was pulled from a polo-shirt pocket and an eager figure darted out, and dashed back to her place.

'Thank you dear, you can take a House Point.'

Ronnie was marched at gunpoint to the head of one line. Half Dorothy's team defected at once.

'Back in your own line, you Greens quick sharp! Right, everybody squat down, hands on hips, elbows out. On the whistle, go! Duckwalk once right round the room, back to the end of the line, then bunnyhop a complete circuit again, and then, Captains only, duckwalk once round again. Got that? First team all home in a nice straight line is the winner!

'I don't believe this,' Ronnie was protesting when the gun forced her to her haunches. Suzy's finger tightened on the trigger. She blew the whistle and jabbed Ronnie behind the ear.

'OK, Sharples. Duckwalk till you drop.'

Ten minutes later, the shop door opened and a policeman announced, 'All clear, ladies. You can come out now.'

But nobody heard him through the clamour and shouts of 'Greens! Greens!' 'Reds! Reds! Reds!' and 'Cheat! Cheat!' as the two big ducklings slugged it out, scarlet-faced and panting, wings pumping, as they waddled for dear life over the chaos of torn books, spilled beer and crackling plastic cups.

The Laughing Academy

After he had closed the door of his mother's flat for the last time McCloud took a taxi to Glasgow airport to catch the shuttle back to London. The driver turned his head and said through the metal grille, 'I know you. You used to be that, ehh . . .' he broke off, not just because he couldn't remember the name but because the burly blond man in the back had his head in his hands and was greeting like a wean, or a boxer who had just lost a fight and knows it was his last. He concentrated on getting through the rush-hour traffic but when a hold-up forced them to a crawl a glance in the mirror showed that the blond curls were tarnished and the cashmere coat had seen better days. As the smell of whisky filtered through, he recognised his passenger as Vincent McCloud the singer. 'Looks like the end of the road for you, pal' he thought. 'The end of the pier.' Re-runs of ancient *Celebrity Squares*, and guesting on some fellow fallen star's *This Is Your Life*; he could see it all, the blazers and slacks and brave Dentu-Creme smiles and jokes about Bernard Delfont and the golf course that only the old cronies in their ill-fitting toupees would get. Like veterans at the Cenotaph they were, their ranks a little thinner every year. That mandatory bit of business they all did, the bear-hugging, backslapping, look-at-you-you-old-rascal, isn't-he-wonderful-ladies-and-gentlemen finger-pointing routine – as if the milked applause could drown the tinkle of coloured lightbulbs popping one by one against the darkness and the desolate swishing of the sea. As the taxidriver pondered on the intrinsic sadness of English showbiz, he thought he remembered that McCloud had been in some bother. Fiddling the taxman, if he minded right. They were all at it.

McCloud was trying not to remember. He'd stood at his mother's bed in the ward, slapping the long thick envelope whose contents brought information about a *Readers' Digest* grand prize draw that her eyes were too dim to read.

'Made it, Ma! Top of the world! This is it, the big yin! A recording contract and an American tour!'

He didn't want to recall all those black and white movies they'd watched together on the television, the smiles and tears of two-bit hoofers and over-the-hill vaudevillians and burlesque queens who were told, 'You'll never play the Palace,' and did. His mother had thought he'd be another Kenneth McKellar.

'That's you, Jimmy.'

McCloud realised that the cab was standing at the airport and the driver was waiting to be paid. Old habits die hard, and McCloud was grateful that the man had failed to recognise him and had not proved to be of a philosophical bent. He gave him a handsome tip.

'Enjoy your flight!' the cabbie called out after him as McCloud went through the door carrying a heavy suitcase of his mother's things.

On his way to the plane McCloud bought a newspaper, a box of Edinburgh rock and a tartan tin of Soor Plooms, acidic boiled sweets which he used to buy in a paper poke when he was a boy. He felt like a tourist. There was nobody left in Scotland for him now.

'Do you mind?' said an indignant English voice.

It seemed he had barged into someone. He glowered. In his heart he had been swinging his fist into the treacherous

119

features of his former manager, Delves Winthrop, that nose that divided into two fat garlic cloves at the tip and the chin with the dark dimple that the razor couldn't penetrate.

'Don't be bitter, Vinny,' Delves had counselled him on the telephone after the trial. 'That's showbiz – you win some, you lose some. Swings and roundabouts. And you know what they say, no publicity is bad publicity . . .'

In that, as in his management of McCloud's career, Delves had been wrong. The Sunday paper which had expressed interest in McCloud's story had gone cold on the idea, and his appearance on *Wogan* had been cancelled at the last minute. Box Office Poison. McCloud, branded more fool than knave, had narrowly escaped prison and bankruptcy, and had – the taxi-driver's surmise had been correct – a guest appearance on a forgotten comedian's *This Is Your Life* to look forward to, and a one-night stand at the De La Warr Pavilion, Bexhill-on-Sea. The small amount of money he'd managed to hold on to was diminishing at a frightening rate.

While McCloud was homing through the gloaming to a flat with rusting green aluminium windows in a vast block in Streatham, Delves was soaking up the sun on the Costa Del Crime with some bikinied floozie. McCloud hoped it would snow on them. Bitter? You bet Vinny was bitter. He sat on the plane contemplating the English seaside in February, his heart a rotting oyster marinated in brackish sea-water. Wormwood and gall, sloes, aloes, lemons were not as bitter. His teeth were set on edge as if by sour green plums. It came to him that Delves Winthrop owned a house on the south coast, not a million miles away from Bexhill.

At Heathrow he lit a cigarette, great for a singer's throat, and telephoned his former wife, Roberta. She was friendly enough at first, and then he lost it.

120

'Is either of the weans with you? I'd like a word.'

'The weans? What is this? Sorting out your mother's things, the perfect excuse to get legless and sentimental, eh Vinny? I might have known you'd come back lapsing into the Doric. I'm glad *we* flew straight back after the funeral.'

'Is Catriona there, or Craig? Put them on, I've a right to speak to them. I'm their father, as far as I know.'

'Ach, away'n bile yer heid, Tammy Troot!' Roberta put the phone down.

Tongue like a rusty razor blade, she'd always had it, since they'd met when he'd been a Redcoat at Butlins at Ayr, and she a holiday-maker hanging round the shows, Frank Codona's funfair it was, thinking herself in love with the greasy boy who worked the waltzer. The Billy Bigelow of Barassie. Well, at least he hadn't gone round to her house, as he'd half intended, the emissary from the Land O' Cakes standing on the doorstep in a tartan scarf to match his breath, with sweeties for his twenty-seven- and twenty-eight-year-olds, the door opened by Roberta's husband. Of course he knew they'd left home years ago. He'd rung on the off chance that one of them might be there. They'd always been closer to their mother.

McCloud let himself into his stale and dusty fourth-floor flat and found two messages waiting on his machine, the first from his daughter Catriona sending love, the second from Stacey, a young dancer he'd been seeing for the past six months.

'Hiya darling, guess what? I got the job!!! Knew you'd be proud of me. Listen babes, we leave on Wednesday so I've got masses to get ready. Oh, hope everything went OK and you're not feeling blue. You know I'd be with you if I could. Call you later. Love you.'

'Dazzle Them at Sea' the ad in the *Stage* had read. Royal Caribbean Cruises. He'd spoken to Stacey yesterday on the phone, just catching her before she trotted off

121

to the audition at the Pineapple Studios in Covent Garden. He could tell from her voice, which sounded as if it were transmitted over miles of ocean by a ship's telephone, that in her heart she was already hoofing under sequined tropical stars.

Her neon-red words hung in the air, then faded as grey silence drifted and extinguished them.

McCloud stowed the bag of his mother's things on top of the wardrobe, feeling guilty at leaving them there but knowing it would be some time before he could bear to look at them. There were objects in that bag he had known all his life, pieces that were older then he was. Desolation suffused him as he stood on the strip of rented carpet. With mother gone, nobody would know who he really was ever again.

He found the copy of the *Stage* and the ad and read it again. Stacey had joined the company of Strong Female Dancers who Sing Well. McCloud could testify to her strength, he thought, but reserved judgement on the singing.

He sat in the living room with framed and unframed posters and playbills stacked against the wall, a glass of whisky in his hand, studying the Directory, the gallery of eccentrics like himself who lived on hope and disappointment: 'Look at me!' they begged, 'Let me entertain you!' Clowns, acrobats, stilt-walkers, magicians, belly-dancers, once-famous pop groups, one-hit wonders, reincarnated George Formbys still cleaning windows, fire-eaters, hilarious hypnotists, Glenn Millers swinging yet and the Dagenham Girl Pipers defying time. Then there were the Look-alikes, fated to impersonate the famous and those whose tragedy lay in a true or imagined resemblance to somebody so faded or obscure that it was inconceivable that the most desperate supermarket manager or stag-night would dream of hiring them. McCloud read on, keeping at bay with little sips of whisky the thought that

122

his own face would soon be grinning desperately there, until he came to the Apartments column.

'Sunny room in friendly Hastings house. Long or short stay. Full English breakfast, evening meal available. Owner in the profession.'

A sunny room in February? McCloud was tempted, although there were three weeks to go before his Bexhill booking. The lime-green fluorescent flyers piled on the table filled him with fear every time they caught his eye, and he worried that his accompanist was going to let him down. The last time he'd seen Joe Ogilvy in the Pizza Express in Dean Street, the boiled blue yolks of his eyes and red-threaded filaments in the whites had not inspired confidence. He could go down and case the joint, get a bit of sea air. He put the thought of Sherry Winthrop, Delves's crazy wife, out of his mind, and dialled the number.

However as he drove down the following morning, crawling along in the old red Cavalier with a windscreen starred by sleet, and Melody Radio, the taxi-drivers' friend, buzzing through the faulty speaker, he imagined Delves's house, to which he had never been invited. Neither had anybody else as far as he knew. It was common knowledge, among those who knew Delves had a wife, that Sherry had been in the bin and she was never allowed to come to London or to be seen in public. She had been Delves's PA, but now he was ashamed of her. She was younger than Delves, of course, and had been quite lively once. In McCloud's mind's eye the Sussex house was tile-hung, its old bricks mellowed with lichen and moss, standing in a sheltered walled garden with a prospect of the sea, and grey-green branches of the southernwood which gave it its name half-hiding the stone toadstools either side of its five-barred gate.

If you listened to Melody Radio, you'd think that love

were all, that the world was full of people falling in love and the sky raining cupid's little arrows. And McCloud liked gutsy songs sung from the heart by people who'd been through the mill, that made you feel life was worth living despite everything. Take the rhinestone cowboy singing now, for example, he hadn't a hope in hell of riding a horse in that star-spangled rodeo, but there he was with his subway token and dollar in his shoe, bloody but unbowed. Tragic if you thought about his future, but it cheered you up, the song. It was not in McCloud's repertoire, he was expected to wester home via the low road to Marie's wedding and his ain folk, but he sang along lustily.

His spirits lifted as he left London's suburbs behind. 'Seagull House, Rock-A-Nore Road, Hastings'; the address had a carefree, striped-candy, rock-a-bye, holiday look about it, and he felt almost as if he were going on holiday with a painted tin spade and pail. The memory of his mother, holding her dress bunched above her bare knees, laughing and running back from the frill of foam at the tide's edge, pulling him with her was more bittersweet than painful, and he resolved to remember only happy times. That was the best he could do for her now. She had told him a poem about fairies who 'live on crispy pancakes of yellow tide-foam,' and he'd tried to remember it for his own children, Catriona and Craig, with their little legs, paddling in their wee stripey pants. Catriona worked in a building society now, and had assured him that it had been for the best, really, that she'd had to leave the Arts Educational Trust when he couldn't find the fees. Craig hadn't found his niche yet and was employed on a casual basis behind the scenes at the National. Great kids, the pair of them. McCloud was not ready yet to admit that whatever he had done as a father was done for good or ill and he was now peripheral to their lives, and the thought of his little girl out in the dark in a dangerous city was

124

too painful to dwell on. He was eager to hit the coast, and so hungry that he could have eaten a pile of those crispy pancakes.

Sherry Winthrop stood at the lounge window of the 1930s bungalow, 'Southernwood'. Flanked by two tall dogs, in her pale-green fluted nightdress with her short auburn hair she might have been a figurine of the period. She was watching the sails of the model windmill on the lawn whirling and whirling in the icy wind, and old gnomes skulking under the shivering bushes. Beyond the front garden's high chain-link fence was a tangle of sloes and briars on a stretch of frostbitten cliff top, narrower every year as boulders of chalk broke off and fell, and beyond that, the sea. A hand on each Dobermann's head, she stood, her mind whirring as purposely as the windmill's sails in the crashing sound of the waves. At length, knowing that she must get dressed and take Duke and Prince for a run, she went to make a cup of coffee. The kitchen, modernised by previous owners and untouched since, was decorated and furnished in late-fifties contemporary style. Sherry would have preferred to go back to bed and lose herself in the murder mystery she was reading but she felt guilty about the dogs' dull lives with her and would force herself for their sakes. Was she not afraid, living alone as she did, to read, late into the night, those gruesome accounts of the fates of solitary women? The dogs were her guards, although sometimes she imagined they might tire of their hostage and kill her, and sometimes she felt it would be almost a relief when the actual murderer turned up at last. There was never one around when you needed him, she had learned. Like plumbers. She just hoped that when he did show up he'd only drug the dogs, not hurt them, and it would be quick and the contents of her stomach not too embarrassing at the autopsy. Had Sherry cared to watch them, her

125

husband's stack of videos would have shown her deeds done to women and children beyond her worst nightmares.

She was conscious of the thin skin of her ankles and her bare feet as she unlocked the back door and let the dogs into the garden. There was a freezer packed with shins and shanks and plastic bags of meat in the garage. Crime novels apart, Sherry was quite partial to stories about nobby people who were always cutting up the dogs' meat and visiting rectors with worn carpets in their studies, and American fiction where they drank orange juice and black coffee in kitchens with very white surfaces.

The time she had needed a murderer most was after she'd lost the baby in an early miscarriage. Delves hadn't wanted children anyway, so he didn't care, and she'd ended up in the bin. It had taken her years to get off the tranquillisers but she was all right now, just half-dead. Sometimes, for no reason, she'd get a peculiar smell in her nose, a sort of stale amyl-nitratey whiff, a sniff of sad, sour institutional air or a thick meaty odour that frightened her. She had woken with it this morning, a taint in the air that made her afraid to open her wardrobe and find it full of stained dressing-gowns.

She would have done something about her life ages ago, if it hadn't been for the dogs. When Delves had brought them home as svelte one-year-olds, they had spied on her and reported her every movement to Delves on portable telephones hidden in their leather muzzles, but Delves had lost all interest in her long since and her relationship with Duke and Prince was much better. It was just that it would be impossible to leave with two great Dobermanns in tow, or towing her. Delves had no wish to remarry – why should he when there was always some girl stupid enough to give him what he wanted – and he said it was cheaper to keep her than divorce her.

There was nothing of the thirties figurine about her

when, in boots and padded jacket, she crunched the gravel path past 'Spindrift', 'South Wind', 'Trade Winds', 'Kitti-wakes', and 'Miramar', with Duke and Prince setting off the dogs in each bungalow in turn.

It was three o'clock when McCloud, having found a parking space, walked up the steep path, through wintry plants on either side and past a rockery where snowdrops bloomed among flints and shells, and rang the bell of Seagull House. It was tall, painted grey with white windows, a deeper grey door, bare wisteria stems, and a seagull shrieking from one of the chimneys. He felt some trepidation now, wishing he'd checked into an anonymous B and B or a sleazy hotel with a scumbag who didn't know him from Adam behind the desk. His fears proved groundless. The ageing Phil Everly look-alike who opened the door showed no sign of recognition. Later, McCloud would learn that he was the remaining half of an Everly Brothers duo whose partner had died recently from AIDS, but for the present Phil simply showed him to a pleasant attic room and asked if he would be in for the evening meal. McCloud decided that he might as well. Left alone, looking out over the jumbled slate and tiled roofs, a few lighted windows and roosting gulls, he wondered what he was doing here. Then he unpacked and walked down to the front and ate a bag of chips in the cold wind among the fishing debris that littered the ground around the old, tall tarred net shops along the Stade. Not very far away, Sherry Winthrop was drifting round Superdrug with an empty basket to the muzak of 'The Girl From Ipanema', avoiding her reflection in the mirror behind the display of sunglasses.

The following day McCloud drove over to Bexhill. Bexhill Bexhill, so good they named it twice. McCloud sat nursing a cup of bitter tea in the cafeteria of the De La Warr

127

Pavilion. He had opened the doors of the theatre and taken a quick look, at the rows of seats and the wooden stage and his throat had constricted, his heart flung itself around in his tight chest and his skin crawled with fear. He had closed the doors quickly on the scene, shabby and terrifying in the February daylight. Then, like the fool he was, clammily he'd asked the woman in the box office how the tickets for the Vincent McCloud show were going.

'Oh, well it's early days yet. Everything's slow just now. Mind you, we were turning people away for Norman Wisdom, but that's different. Anyhow, we can usually rely on a few regulars who'll turn out for anything. Did you want to book some seats?' she concluded hopefully.

McCloud sat among the scattering of elderly tea-drinkers, his prospective audience if he were lucky, with *Let's call the whole thing off* going through his head. The woman in the box office must have taken him for a loony. Maybe he was. Maybe that's where he was headed, the Funny Farm. He saw the inmates racing round a farm-yard in big papier-mâché animal heads, butting each other mirthlessly and falling over waving their legs in the air. Or the Laughing Academy. He'd heard the bin called that too, a grander establishment obviously, and then he remembered reading of someone setting up a school for clowns. He pictured the Laughing Academy as a white classical building with columns, and saw its pupils sitting at rows of desks in a classroom with their red noses, all going 'Ha ha ha ha, ho ho ho' like those sinister mechanical clowns at funfairs. He cursed Delves Winthrop for all the bookings not made, the poor pub-licity, the wasted opportunities, the wonky contracts, the criminally negligent financial management, and he cursed himself for not having broken away while his voice and his hair was still golden. He thought about Norman Wisdom who travelled with his entourage in a forty-seater luxury coach, with a cardboard cut-out of himself

128

propped up in one of them, and he remembered the child, a mini-Norman look-alike in a 'gump suit' who followed Norman round the country with his parents, and speculated on their weird family life; father driving, mother stitching a new urchin cap for the boy's expanding head and the kid in the back working on his dimples, mentally rehearsing a comic pratfall; a star waiting to be born. The hell with it. He was down, but not out yet. McCloud finished his tea, stubbed out his cigarette and went out into the sea fog which had swirled up suddenly, and found a ticket on his windscreen. He had forgotten to pay and display.

When he had arrived he had been momentarily cheered by the De La Warr Pavilion, that Modernist gem rising above the shingle with its splendour damaged but not entirely gone, the white colonnade and the odd houses with their little domes and minarets and gardens and white painted wooden steps, but now he saw that Bexhill-on-Sea was a town without pity. He bought a bottle of whisky and drove back to Hastings.

Phil was in the hall of Seagull House talking to a woman with a little dog.

'Let me introduce you' he said. 'Mr McCloud – Miss Bowser, and her schnauzer Towser. Miss Bowser has the flatlet on the first floor.'

Beatrix Bowser, a gaunt grizzled girl in her sixties with hair like a wind-bitten coastal shrub, wearing a skirt and jersey, held out a rough, shy hand.

'I did so enjoy hearing you sing that lovely old Tom Moore song on *Desert Island Discs* recently, Mr McCloud,' she said gruffly, and fled upstairs with the little grinning brindled chap at her heels.

'Is she in the profession?' asked McCloud, imagining a novelty act with Towser wearing a paper ruff and pierrot

129

cap whizzing round the stage accompanied by Miss Bowser on the accordion.

'Retired schoolmistress. Classics. Beatrix is one of the old school. I'm sorry, should I have recognised you?'

'No.' McCloud said. 'I'm out for dinner, by the way.'

On the way to his room he took a glass from the bathroom, and he poured himself a shot and lay on his bed thinking about the grip of Stacey's strong dancer's legs.

The sea fog seeped through 'Southernwood's windows and the dogs were restless in the dank, chilly air, making Sherry uneasy with their pacing, clicking claws on the lino as she lay in bed reading.

'Settle down, you two!' she commanded. 'Come on, up on the bed with Mummy!' She patted the old peach-coloured eiderdown. As she did, the dogs hurled themselves towards the front door barking dementedly. Sherry froze in terror. The doorbell rang. The dogs were going mad, leaping and battering the door. The murderer had come and she didn't want him. The bell sent another charge through her rigid body. Unable to move, to creep to the telephone, she sat upright, praying that the dogs would frighten him off.

A man's voice came through the door, distorted by the barking. Sherry looked round wildly for a weapon, her mind lurching towards the back door, the garden fence and the flight through darkness to 'Spindrift', seeing herself beating on its door while its inhabitants, as she had done, cowered in fear, refusing to open. Feeling the hands round her throat.

'Vincent McCloud – ' The voice was snapped off by the letterbox and dogs' teeth.

Half-aware of feeling like someone in a film, Sherry slid her legs to the floor, and slipped on her dressing-gown. The front door was unlocked and opened a crack.

130

McCloud saw a bit of her face, a brass poker, two thrusting muzzles with the upper lip lifted over snarling teeth.

'I'm terribly sorry to disturb you. Can I come in a minute?'

'Friend!' said Sherry, keeping the dogs, who had no conception of the word, at bay with the poker. 'Lie down!'

Slavering, they sank growling to the floor.

'Delves isn't here,' Sherry said. 'In fact he's hardly ever here. What do you want?'

'Oh – I was just passing.' McCloud attempted a disarming grin.

'Pull the other one,' said Sherry, tightening the belt of her dressing gown. 'If you're hoping to get at Delves by doing anything to me, forget it. I'm his least valued possession.'

'I wasn't, I swear. Look, the truth is, I had to be in Bexhill and I thought I'd look you up. And take a look at the Winthrop lifestyle, I must admit.'

'Well, now you've seen it. Bit different from what you expected, eh? The heart of the evil empire. You might have telephoned first.'

'And you'd have told me not to come. Look, here's my bona fides.' He took a lime-green flyer announcing his concert from his pocket.

Sherry studied it and handed it back without comment. She was beginning to experience an odd, long-forgotten sense of having the upper hand, and enjoying it.

'Do you want a drink?' she asked. 'Before you go. Another drink, perhaps I should say.'

They were sitting in the front room, Sherry with her feet tucked up under her on the sofa, and McCloud in a chair. A bottle of Cloudy Bay stood opened on the table, a rectangular slice of onyx on curlicued gilt legs. McCloud put out a tentative hand to Prince, who didn't bite it off.

'This is Delves's wine,' Sherry said. 'I don't often touch his precious cellar. It's too dangerous, living on your own.

131

And it's horrible replacing it. I feel so guilty that I'm sure they think I'm an alckie, and if they think you really need the stuff, they just fling it at you without even a bit of coloured tissue round it. That blue tissue always makes me think of fireworks – light the blue touch paper and retire. Sorry, I'm rabbiting on. I'm not used to having anyone to talk to and I got a bit carried away.'

'It's nice to hear you talk. We never got a chance to get to know each other, did we?'

'No. But I never get the chance to know anybody. People round here keep themselves to themselves, well, I suppose I do too. I've sort of lost touch with my family. After I was ill, you know, after I – my baby – well, I think they were embarrassed, didn't know what to say to me. And they never liked Delves. Or vice versa.'

As Vincent clicked the table-lighter, an onyx ball, at a cigarette, Sherry was thinking that she might get in touch now. Suddenly she missed them dreadfully. McCloud was thinking how pretty she looked, now that the wine and the gas fire had flushed her pale face. He was thinking too that, if he drank any more, he wouldn't be able to drive. He'd had a good snort or two before setting out, as Sherry had noticed.

'May I?' He refilled their glasses.

'Do you want some stale nuts or crisps?'

'That would be nice. I am a bit hungry.'

'I could make you a sandwich. It will have to be Marmite.'

'My favourite,' said McCloud.

'Vincent,' she said, as he ate his sandwiches, 'Are you on your own? I mean, is there anybody in your, you know, life?'

He shook his head. 'There was, a girl, a dancer. She was young enough to be my daughter. I don't know what she saw in me. Well, not much, evidently.'

Sherry's dislike of the glamorous nubile cavorter was

132

appeased when Vincent added, 'A two-bit hoofer who'll never play the Palace.'

He found himself telling Sherry about his mother, and how he had deceived her about the recording contract.

'I wanted to make her happy. Or proud of me. I don't really know for whose sake I did it. Anyway, either she can see me and know the truth, or she can't.'

'She would just want you to be happy. And I bet she *was* proud of you.'

Vincent saw his young self against a painted backdrop of loch and mountains. 'Och, aye,' he said flatly. 'Look, Sherry, I ought to be going. After all, I got you out of bed.' A deep blush overtook the rosy flush on her face. Motes of embarrassment swarmed in the air around them, settling on her dressing-gown.

'You shouldn't really be driving. You must be over the limit.'

'Probably.'

'There is a spare room. Only we'd have to air some sheets. Everything gets really damp here. I think it's the sea. Everything rusts.' Including me, she thought, not knowing if she wanted him to make a move towards her. She knew she was lousy in bed. Delves had told her.

'May I really stay? Thank you. Please don't worry about the sheets, I'm sure I've slept in worse.'

'I could give you a hot-water bottle.'

'Real men don't use hot-water bottles. Have you got any music? The night's still young.'

He flicked through the few albums. Tape and CD had not arrived at 'Southernwood'. He held out his arms. They danced awkwardly, to 'La vie en rose', watched by the dogs with Duke howling along to the song.

'They think we've gone mad,' said Sherry, invoking a memory of the bin, and remembering her own inadequacy. She broke away from Vincent and sat down abruptly.

133

'Look, Sherry, I don't know what upset you but I'm sorry.' He was disturbed by the feel of her body through the dressing gown and nightdress. She shivered at the loss of his body close to her.

'If you think I was trying to use you to get back at Delves, you're quite, quite wrong. This is nothing whatsoever to do with him.' He knelt beside her and took her hand. 'We'll leave it for tonight. Maybe we can go out somewhere tomorrow. Would you like that?'

Sherry nodded. Then remembered that she had started out calling the shots and said, 'We'll take the dogs to Camber and give them a good run over the sands. OK?' she added a little uncertainly.

'Fine. And I'll take you out to lunch.'

He dismissed the thought of his dwindling bank balance, and realised he should call Seagull House, to let them know he hadn't done a runner or gone over a cliff.

Sometime later, lying wakefully with his cold hot-water bottle in sheets that smelled faintly mildewed, having refused a pair of Delves's damp pyjamas and wearing the tartan boxer shorts Stacey had given him – 'Tartan breath' was one of her names for him – he sensed his door opening slowly. Sherry. Two shapes leapt through the gloom and landed on the bed and made themselves comfortable either side of him.

'Thanks, boys. You're pals.'

He eased himself out and padded to Sherry's room. 'The dogs have taken over my bed,' he said, shutting the door behind him.

She was soft and warm as he took her in his arms, and inert. He kissed her gently and then harder when a fluttering response came from her lips.

'I don't do this . . .' she struggled to say.

'No. Only with me.'

'I've forgotten how. Rusty . . .' she was saying into his

134

mouth, feeling herself to be as attractive as an old gate. She was warm and soft. His lips grazed breasts like little seashells just visible in the darkness. They made love gently. It was nothing like being in bed with Stacey, he thought, which sometimes felt more like an aerobics session than passion.

'I thought you'd forgotten how,' he teased her, and said, 'You are quite wonderful, and beautiful.'

After a late breakfast of toast and Marmite they drove to Camber. A pair of firecrests flashed past them, bright against dun tangles as they climbed the path between prickly bushes to the dunes.

'Oh look, aren't they pretty!' said Sherry. Then she screamed. She saw a dead bird impaled on the thorns, and then another and another. All around them hundreds of little birds were stuck on the thorns, netted in the wire diamonds of a broken fence; grey-brown sodden masses of feathers glued and pinned to every bush.

'What's the matter?'

She was paralysed with horror. 'We've got to go back!'

'Why?'

'Can't you see them? Look! Everywhere. Songbirds. Trapped. Please, please, we've got to get out of here!' She was crying, tugging his arm violently.

As he saw them it flashed through Vincent's mind that this was some horrible local custom perpetrated by the people who owned the closed pub they had passed and he felt that they were in an evil, barren place. Then he looked harder as the dogs came bounding back to find them.

'They're not birds, darling! Look! They're some sort of, of natural, vegetable phenomenon. Cast up by the sea perhaps, just bits of – matter, dead foliage or something.'

Sherry was not convinced. The shape and colour of them were so dead-birdlike. Vincent pulled one off a bush.

'See?'

It lay, disgusting, in his hand. She did see now that the matted hanks had never been birds, but still the place seemed the scene of a thousand crucifixions. She was trembling with the thorny impact of it. Vincent wrapped the two sides of his coat round her, pulling tightly to his chest.

'"Come, rest in this bosom, my own stricken deer, Though the herd have fled from thee, thy home is still here."' Then he said, 'You're frozen. Come back to Seagull House with me. There are some kind people there, and then we can decide what we're going to do next.'

And there's a little dog, he realised, but decided to worry about that when they got there. They walked back past the shuttered chalets and beach shops to the car, Vincent trying not to think about the De La Warr Pavilion, shuddering at the image of himself on the stage, hanging on to the mike for support, belting out 'My Way' '"Regrets, I've had a few . . ."' and a heckling voice shouting 'More than a few, mate!' Maybe he would give the rest of the whisky to Phil or Miss Bowser. Sherry was suddenly reminded of an afternoon near Christmas some years ago when she had delivered some presents to her sister's house. The three children had been sitting in a row on the sofa with a big bowl on the low table in front of them, threading popcorn on strings for the birds. Like children in a story book, except they were watching television. The picture of them made her happy.